MY DOUBLE IDENTITIES AS HUNTER & DETECTIVE AND OUTCAST & VICTIM

Lars Werner

WORKBOOK PRESS LLC

187 E Warm Springs Rd,

Suite B285, Las Vegas, NV 89119, USA

Website:	https://workbookpress.com/
Hotline:	1-888-818-4856
Email:	admin@workbookpress.com

Ordering Information:

Quantity sales. Special discounts are available on quantity purchases by corporations, associations, and others.

For details, contact the publisher at the address above.

Library of Congress Control Number:

ISBN-13:	978-1-960752-97-0 (Paperback Version)
	978-1-960752-98-7 (Digital Version)

REV. DATE: 06/12/2023

MY DOUBLE IDENTITIES AS HUNTER & DETECTIVE AND OUTCAST & VICTIM

The Compilation of Works of Agent Lars Werner

5937 APPENDIX VIII 347:
<u>Economics as a Science Phenomenon</u>

Queen Elizabeth II: 'Yes, and what about your conclusion top-agent 027 Warner Bond?'

I as 027 Bond: 'Now, sensible grown-ups around the world have finally developed a so-called ecological climate-strategy which they can unite behind… and then some smart and cunning Swedish businessmen around new green technology will destroy consensus xxx around the whole world about a strategy to reach Paradise on Planet Earth and these Swedish businessmen is using Greta Thunberg as a bait or lure in their marketing. Hm, we must remember 11/9 2001 and Usama bin Laden being a Swedish friend and there were holds on Sweden being caused by the Swedish Active Neutrality-Policy for example being caused during the eighties and nineties and here I have mentioned examples: Hm, I am not sure that some Swedish plans of World-dominator has been put on some shelf,.. Yet. Oh, there has been some Germans visiting Sweden, lately.

Queen Elizabeth II: 'Well, I guess I should talk with Boris Johnson about Swedish plans of domination or (world) domination. Maybe Swedes have not only dubious relations with our fishy French for mentors, but they have also special relations with the Germans officially visiting Sweden now in a whispering way behind official protocols and The Russkies are always around in some in official ways also exporting military equipment and arrays assisted by submissions and this was especially common during the eighties. Hm, and submarine were perhaps use active during the nineties political charms were not only political virgins and Swedes were incompetent chasing Russian submarine. Hm, and the Chinese and deepwater-technology and Geely and Li Shufen... And the growing Chinese market is big and growing where opportunities can be found for Swedes. Yes, all this I can't say officially. I then of course have to deny officially what I have said in officially.'

I as 027 Bond and Noman Sheleton: 'My authorship will most likely be described by the Swedish prime minister as an infamous and deliberate attack towards the Swedish World-Conscience, or who only to dominate the World by only unselfish deeds.... Not true... Since I have in my authorship shown a number of criminal deeds made by the Swedes and Swede are also often looking for power and influence.'

5938 APPENDIX VIII 348:
<u>Economics as a Science Phenomenon</u>

Queen Elizabeth II: 'Well, I happen to know that the Swedish Parliament made the Swedish king powerless 1974, without asking the Swedish people about it. Furthermore, I now also happen to know about Swedish crimes and also possible Swedish crimes you have written about 027 Bond and Nomen Skeleton. Oh, Swedish journalists do now know about your case 027 Bond and Noman Skeleton and so do now also the whole Swedish Parliament, but they do not inform the Swedish people about Nomen Skeleton's existence, but selected people around the world are also informed about my existence. Yes, it is interesting to know that the MPS of the Swedish Parliament do think that it is necessary to inform the Swedish people about the existence of Nomen Skeleton and his authorship and it is also interesting to know that Swedish journalist do keep quiet about Nomen Skeleton's authorship. Yes, I consider myself informed about the Swedish so-called democracy and to some extent I am amused, but to be amused about the anti-Democratie relation between the Swedish Parliament and the traditional Swedish Mass-Media and not do anything about it is most shameful.'

I as 027 Bond and Nomen Skeleton: Exactly! Yes, but it was some kind of experiment and now there are, I believe, discussions between U.S.A. and China about the publisher Gui Minhai being in some "house-arrest in China and being both a Swedish citizen and a Chinese citizen – and he knows about Swedish dissidents writing book-manuscripts like me. Now, this Gui Minhai could be a publisher to a Swedish dissident like me for example in China linked to some extent to maybe Workbook press in U.S.A. well, sometimes agreements may come true. Hm, but Swedish Media have helped me with some information... Due to some pressure from the American being interested in so-called mor or less Natural Experiments – being related more *or* less in secret to a so-called Nobel Prize... X-files.'

5939 APPENDIX VIII 349:
<u>Economics as a Science Phenomenon</u>

Queen Elizabeth II: 'Anything else?'

I as 027 Bond replied: 'Well, some battery factories are planned in the north of Norway and in the town of vasa in the North of Finland... and here we can talk about... two new competitors and battery-factories., suddenly appearing., which perhaps could see to it that the Swedish battery-factory in the North at Sweden in the town of Skellefled had made over-investments well, the old method "Divide and Rule" had first been applied by the Swedes in the matrix-game between Sweden & Partners and USA & Partners related to Democrats and Republicans and a hostage and then now here it probably was an American Battery-game which the Swedes from the start were not aware of thinking that they had a monopoly-situation due to a hostage, a monopoly-situation which then disappeared when Swedes had done calculated investments, but then the situation changed when competitive business-actors arrived in the Northern parts of Norway and Finland. Hm, the old method, "Divide and Rule". Yes, Swedish over-investments...'

Queen Elizabeth II: 'Now, the general question is why does Sweden has such a good reputation within the EU-family of nations while Poland and Hungry has such a bad reputation. I am sure you have a scientific answer to this question based on empiric data, top-agent or Warner Bond, Noman Skeleton also is related to your being. Now, can you answer that my question.'

I as 027 Warner Bond & Noman-Skeleton answered.' Sure... Since Sweden contribute to the joint EU- Budget while Poland and Hungary do constitute more or less great drains on the joint EU-budget., and furthermore, Sweden does also contribute to the joint EU-budget through black hostage-taking and thereby the taxation-basis (the stock of milk-cow capacity) will increase and therefore Sweden is a heroin for example the EU-commission.'

3940 APPENDIX VIII 350:
<u>Economics as a Science Phenomenon</u>

Queen Elizabeth II: 'Hm, our Lord in heaven must sometimes be in a state of mind where he has many misgivings about the Human Race. Doomsday is around the corner. I now have some fear that there is no hope for Mankind anymore. Mankind can't escape!!! The Holy Prophet Moses will come down from the Mountain-top with the tablets of The Ashine laws for the whole Mankind, and if Mankind have objections, then Mankind will vanish from the surface of the Planet Earth.'

I as 027 Werner Bond and Noman Skeleton now answered with a possible alternative outcome for sinful Mankind saying,' Well, there is only one hope left for Mankind and that is if first U.S.A. and China will come to an agreement related to ecological matters on this Planet Earth which then embrace/comprise climate matters and where the big outlets of CO2 are of vital importance. There are methods and equipment which can suck in CO2-molecules and divide CO2-molecules causing a negative economic growth when it comes to the presence/part of CO2-molecules in the atmosphere and the costs are affordable to Mankind and then there are Chimmies related to factories etc. who are equipped with filters which can stop a positive growth of the part of CO2-molecules in the atmosphere around the Globe on Planet Earth and also hydro-electric power-stations shouldn't be a threat to fish-animals and their living-conditions and their ways to reach some open SE2 and there are a lot of investments here to be done while waiting for the transition-process from fossil energy (oil + CO2/+ gas) and nuclear energy to sustainable energy (water + wind + sun-beams),.. But this process will take some time… and during this time of process big corporations like Exxon oil etc. Can invest in less developed countries who do.

5941 APPENDIX VIII 351:
<u>Economics as a Science Phenomenon</u>

I need not only power-stations distributing electricity in a more sustainable way... but who also do need other investment-objects of competitive nature and therefore could be integrated in the global economy. Now, this means new investments-opportunities for cooperations moving from business in fossil energy to other kinds of business including also mostly sustainable energy and then also business-corporations within "the industrial-military-complex" do need strategies to expand one global market and then there will be both money and know-how from big international corporations going into less developed countries while the whole world will face a process of economic integration into...

"The Global Union of States". If U.S.A. and China can come to a special certain agreement of Global understanding... then "some still less integrated European Union in the making" "some still poor union of India being in a process of modernization will follow after... and then Mankind have internet where people can meet and discuss in groups etc. And then also do we have super-fast vehicles in vacuum-tunnels moving with a speed of ten times the speed of sound – and with all these things to work with then Mankind will need a Global Union. Hm, national police-forces can't chase criminals around "The Globe" and we can't let nations to go on and Declaire war to each other!'

Queen Elizabeth II: 'Hm, you have told me that you have been exposed to a combat-experiment what do you mean by that, great top-agent 027 Warner Bond?'

I as 027 Bond answered: 'There was a belting-game around me as Noman Skeleton, I think. Yes, that I as one of the last could be one of the first... Hm, why? Well, I had some potential... and I assume this was me guess or hypothesis.'

5942 APPENDIX VIII 352:
<u>Economics as a Science Phenomenon</u>

I as 027 Bond continued: 'Yes, a combat experiment where one gang was Sweden & Partners, and another gang was U.S.A. & Partners or rather an anti-thesis. Yes, and Sweden & Partners had a hypothesis that I should remain to be one of the last while the other gang U.S.A & Partners had the opposite hypothesis being the last to become one of the first because of the very fact that I had the potential! Yes, I was a test person who could be a loser, because I was depending on my weaknesses, and I wasn't in the position to capitalize/ make use of my abilities, and this anti hypothesis was the hypothesis of anti-Sweden & Partners – and in a certain situation, I could fail! Yes, but I could also be a test person who could be a winner, because when I wasn't depending on my weaknesses, and if I was in a position to make use of my abilities then I could be a winner. Yes, in this certain situation, I could be victorious … and here I was backed by U.S.A & Partners who believed in the thesis in let's say some biblical way!

Yes, and when I belonged to one of the last who had become one of the first! Well, I was a test person who had to face different kinds of technologies of less visible administrative control which could include different kinds of violence", but not direct physical violence, I guess. Hm, I had the choice to be oriented toward a human being linked to "The Dark Primitive Human Nature", but as an author, I felt that I should look to the future and therefore I was oriented towards "The Moral and Analytical Advanced Human Nature". Now, I was a test person related to logic-thinking & creativity creating practical innovations. Hm, administration of different innovations where books also could be innovations! Hm, some kind of strange experiment being related to a serial such experiments, I think finding out about human subjects, I think!

5943 APPENDIX VIII 353:
<u>Economics as a Science Phenomenon</u>

I as 027 Bond paused and added: 'Hm, I suppose we here are talking about an administration of innovative thinking... where when success than the thesis was proven and bonds will be signed linked to the U.S.A. & Partners... and Sweden & Partners will be punished for hostage-taking and extortion and criminal gains having formulated the anti-thesis... while U.S.A & Partners have formulated the thesis being proven.'

Queen Elizabeth II: 'Gosh! Administration of innovative thinking and probabilities of prophecies related to some thesis and anti-thesis by non-actors being independent experts & experimentalists and their sureness.'

Lawyer Tea-Taffany Game Feller: 'Well, "Truth or Consequence" is one device/motto while "Truth and consequence" is another device/motto. Right now, I prefer "Truth and Consequence". Gosh!'Prophet Moses: 'Well, then I am connected to this lady and lawyer Tea-Taffany Game Feller, making me happy!'Jesus Christ: 'Yes, but the Swedes didn't want to risk more than a loss of their good reputations... and therefore I have to forgive them, these Swedes.'

Queen Elizabeth II: 'Hm, but I think the Swedes underestimated you 027 Bond being then some kind of Devine agent. However, the Swedish King – and the Swedish people had no say in the matter. Oh, and nor does the Swedish Prime Minister have to ask for help from the almighty! Yes, and look now at what has happened with Sweden! Well, Sweden has now entered a place where all hope has gone.'

5944 APPENDIX VIII 354:
<u>Economics as a Science Phenomenon</u>

Fatso Bullit: 'Well, I know that I place... and I am happy to guide the Swedish World-Conscience down there at least in the first four/eight circles of hell as Dante has known them in his revelation.'

John Milton: 'There is a road to Paradise used for those who do believe in God or The Almighty.'

Fatso Bullit: 'Yes, but let us first visit a boxing match between Adam Smith and Karl Marx...

Where we will talk to them between the boxing rounds.' Adam Smith: 'Hard competition is a driving force behind innovations.'Karl Marx: 'Yes, and hard competition is also a driving force behind industrial espionage and extortion leading to the black cooperation deals... and rationalizations leading to unemployment – some good things will lead to some bad things and people will always complain.'

Adam Smith: 'Yes, there will be complaints, but then there is something called result moral.'

John Milton: 'Yes, and as I have understood it – the brutal system of capitalism both has and will create – the infrastructure of paradise. Yes, a paradise here on this planet Earth instead of a paradise in heaven... but we all still have to wait for this heaven to come true on this planet Earth.'

I as 027 Bond replied: 'Yes, and some people are tired to wait for

paradise arriving to planet Earth since when I asked them to do that,
I just got a black eye.'

5945 APPENDIX VIII 355:
<u>Economics as a Science Phenomenon</u>

Karl Marx: 'Yes, you got a black eye from a young chap with difficulties to fit in... into the Swedish society and be wanted things to be fixed immediately, at once and promptly... and then he couldn't find any other way out then the criminal way... and "The Dark Primitive Human Nature" did dominate him... and no competent human being was around helping him... No competent fellow of "The Moral and Analytica Advanced Human Nature" was around helping him, because it shouldn't lead to good enough results. Yes, the very result moral had them spoken... and every (young) fellow couldn't be helped within the framework of capitalism. Yes, we have to wait for the infrastructure of a social Global Paradise being...built up by capitalistic societies and also economically integrated by capitalistic societies. I have also got a black eye from an angry young lad being tired to wait for a legal chance when I told him he just had to wait 200 years or so... and then I had to join fast socialists and criticize well-meaning over-class ladies who wanted to damp down the misery of poor people and unemployed people etc. In some true Christian Spirit and then I began to talk about revolution and such things and... then I didn't get any blacker eye.'

I said: 'Well, anyway... you know that I have been inside an experiment and there I made my analysis unlike those experimentalists being outside the experiment like a professor Subway Sweetie Pie and Professor Hunter Mabon.' Now, Karl Marx had to go back to the seventy-five rounds in the boxing game of the champ-title meeting Adam Smith.'

Stockholm,

2019-05-20

Hej Lars,

Vi har nu läst och diskurterat ditt manus "My double identities as Hunter & Detective and Outcast & Victim" och har tyvärr bestlutat att tacka nej till att representera verket, trots många fina kvaliteer.

Du skriver bra och medryckande, och det är en spännande historia.

Men, vi tar oss an ca 1-2 nya författarskap per år och för att vi ska kunna motivera en utlandssatsning krävs det ett verk som vi brinner för till hundra procent. Där upplevde vi inte att ditt verk nådde hela vägen fram.

Tack för att vi fick chans att läsa och stort lycka till med boken och ditt fortsatta författarskap.

Bästa hälsningar,

Cecilia

S

Cecilia Imberg

Manusläsare

Salomonsson Agency

Götgatan 27

116 21 Stockholm Sweden Tel: +46 (0) 8 22 32 11

Email: cecilia@salomonssonagency.com

Internet: www.salomonssonagency.com

Table of **CONTENTS**

PREFACE

My first book is entitled My Double Identities as Hunter & Detective and Outcast & Victim. This talks about Noman Skeleton who is the first to trust the Americans more than he should and then have to leave the university as a failure... and this was unfair, but maybe a good experience – empiric data!

Those identities do refer to 027 Warner Bond and Noman.

Skeleton in my book texts describing my experiences and what was going on in the less lawful society where some persons are invented and some persons have other names and in this way, I push the story forward which happen to take place in a certain BAD Department in a certain University of Monte Fresco where I had become a test-person without my knowledge and then I left the University but not my situation as a test-person. Yes, I became aware of being a test-person writing books.

All About the Author:

The author is born in 1946 as the only child in marriage. My father was a single mail carrier, and my mother watched children when working, so I was from a low-class social background. But my grandfather was a physician, which meant that my father had gone downwards the social ladder which made him carry a psychological wound which influenced me towards right-wing extremism for some time being ridiculous, but I was never organized, then father died when I was 20 years old.

I passed a University exam in business administration, but when working, I was slow and not accurate. I succeeded to get a relief work at the Department of Business Administration where I did some temporary works. I passed some courses and I was accepted as a candidate for the doctorate, but then all of my project suggestions were refused. That's when I began to write a number of linked book manuscripts related to my own project.

Chapter 1
ORGANIZED BLINKING LIGHT-TOWERS

Overwhelmed by all things new and recent experience being brought upon me, I fell asleep nearby the Mill-Shore of ÅrstaCreek. I finally awoke after 12-15 hours of deep sleep, and just when I had awoken... I rubbed the sand out of my eyes... I now suddenly saw Strudel Heruaslinken walking towards at the beach. She was wearing brown "Leader-hosen" and she did know how to yodel, which she did when she saw me... a strange carmensita who now also told me that she was of sinful stock, being born out of wedlock. Until now Strudel Herauslinken had been living in Asuncion, with her germ-strange father – Adolfo Agusto Herauslinken, a man from the old school.

When this strange and very sinful kind of girl or young woman named Strudel Herauslinken now undressed and changed to a small bikini, then I got butterflies in my stomach. In my very silence, I repeated the phrase "No unnecessary sex, please, I am a secret agent", and I did it over and over again around me, despite summertime.

I looked at Strudel and then after some discussion about problems with her mixed cultural background... I told her about a pilot study of mine. I now "suggested" that Strudel should study that communication –pattern around Mr. Edby. That Edby-fellow who knew certain interesting facts about computers and energy-power, like nuclear power. I was now surprised when this young woman Strudel Herauslinken... just smiled, and then told me that she already had mapped that very pattern of relations and communications which I now just had mentioned... that communication pattern around Mr. Edby. For instance Mr. Edby's relations to DDR, the Department of Defense Research. There Mr. Edby could run into Brita Schwarz was also around at the BAD cupboard Department, I remembered. I could see her now and then there. Gee, Guran Edby and Brita Schwarz and ASEA-Atom.

Hm, I knew about Edby's relation to that energy-company ASEA, and I therefore, saw to it that Strudel Herauslinken in a systematic way should be studying different companies, and especially ASEA, different decent departments, and different holders. Again, I was surprised when Strudel Herauslinken told me that she already was working with a list... of Edby's relations. I wondered if Rut Link had something to do with all this? Why should I as "boss and führer" instruct women to do things already know what to do?!

I said: 'My,… you are a clever girl who carry out many a work task in advance,… and now you must have base to start from, some event or some discovery. Strudel: 'Oh, there are some discussions about a deal for ASEA going east, but I don't know if those negotiations are serious or not.'

I said: 'Yes, depending on what kind of order these ASEA people do argue about... you can encircle the right departments like those departments of purchase and sales. You then also have to find out who have what kind of authority, what kind of work-task, what kind of personnel connections.'

Now I could see the head of this Yoke Coursesackoh who was coming down the hill... from this ÅrstaWindmill. The head was coming nearer. Hm, Yoke didn't caught sight of me and Strudel. Yoke now stopped and rolled out her blanket. Oh, when she now undressed, she probably thought I did not see her. I used some opera glasses. Strudel had, however, closed her eyes. Finally, Yoke Coursesackoh had her bikini on. I now went to Yoke and told her where I and Strudel were. Now Yoke suddenly gave me a grim face calling me a birdwatcher. Birdwatcher? Had Yoke really seen me with my opera-glasses? Was I a man of a filthy mind, also?'

I watched Yoke's face. Yes, she had passed the beauty operation. She was of Mongolian race and now she had reinforced or sharpened some vague Western features of face and body. Nice personal mix of West and East, I thought. I put my arm around her… but Yoke was angry and once again she called me birdwatcher and told me that her father had got so angry during "The Hot Global World War", that her father and his brothers-in-arms were eating or had 48 American soldiers for dinner, leaving only the Skeleton left – and then she added that some Japanese didn't mind eating up yet another white fellow for dinner. Tora-tora-tora! I was confused.

Finally, I turned over to Strudel, and I put my arm around her, but had quickly to withdraw it... I said: "Strudel, let's be serious, and being serious I come to think of it, a big company like ASEA is no doubt involved in some criminal business, criminal business which may lead to... that this company ASEA might let some people outside the company take care of... yes some kind of dark ASEA will probably let those outsiders do the dirty work for them as contractors."

Yoke, Strudel, and me... now still lay on a blanket and wondered about this strange world and why not everybody could act normal like us, and we did wonder in a philosophical way! Finally, I gave my arms around the two girls, but then they went for a swim and some diving activities, yelling: 'No unnecessary sex, please! We are now secret agents and secret agent seekers!'

After some kind of refreshing break, then I and the two girls also had some picnic. Soured milk, cornflakes, egg and bacon, coffee, bread and butter not to mention the final dish. During this refreshing break; Strudel and Yoke now showed me a photo of a Black negro jail-customer in the nude with a very big black cock, ready to act. His name was Hortone I.S Loose. He showed a message in which said, "Call me when you need me".

I now understood that these two smart female junior journalists were paid to used Hortone as an access-arm to get information in their hard work as journalists. The access arm was a very big black cock. Those two girls did profit a lot on Hortone... and profits were then shared between those two female journalists, Yoke and Strudel... and the governor-warden named Mr. Luvebeer. Oh, all those people with a corrupt soul! Hortone's benefit was nothing but sexual satisfaction since he was unaware of that profit –sharing game above his head.

Yes, Hortone who was put in jail because of planted evidence being all false and from that jail-position this Hortone should and must give first-class sex service to women! Hm, and for his fine supply of sex service... Hortone was miserably paid. Gee, Hortone was controlled by some Swedish union, a union which however didn't acknowledge Hortone's true trade. Still, in criminal negotiations these union-men LeoBodyswap and Strule North were outstanding.

Oh, Swedish unions and sex service and Hortone gets nothing despite the fact that he was controlled by Swedish union – always speaking fair share. I scratched my hair and told Strudel and Yoke that they really had got something there and I also told them that I was very impressed, although I felt sorry for the sexy young black male who was used in some unfair way, because he didn't get this fair share of his sexy and spy-see/spicy activities. I therefore shouted: 'Someone should defend his rights!'

For some reason which I will never understand these two girls just giggled. Who was funny? Me or that black guy? Young women ought to understand that this life is not a funny game! Especially not for those ones who have to face a prison situation or a hostage-like situation or industrial espionage. I got suddenly very angry, but thanks to my male upbringing... I was able to control myself. Sometimes cruel sufferings look funny!

I now suddenly just took Yoke Coursesackoh aside, and when I did, I talked to her about this Dr. Nicholas and his fast and present appointment... for an acting professorship in Finland. I told Yoke to look into this affair. She in her turn now gave me a written message from Rut Link. I then did some reading and said no more.

I just arose and picked up my recently bought Lewis Jeans which I never had worn before and then I just walked away, and while doing so I now could feel how those two girls really did admire me and really yaaarned for my body? Levis Jeans, irresistible since 1853.

I now again looked at that message, a piece of paper, from Rut Link. She wrote that I should meet Roy Carson at Årsta Windmill at a certain time. I now came just in time thanks to my Rolex watch. I went to the windmill and did see that Irish, middle age "gentleman?" I now did just as Roy Carson and ordered some Irish coffee. This special Irish coffee was the secret sign which was supposed to release a discussion between me and Roy Carson. Yes, there was a discussion between me and Carson's junior journalists being dwarfs. I got some phone numbers to a strange town named Kidstone. Hm, I had all my identity papers as Mr. Jones... with me. I now therefore at once went to Arlanda Airport outside Stockholm.

I now went by air to Kidstone in U.S.A, and during an intermediary landing I called for a meeting at that famous hotel, "Waiting Hearts"... situated at Playhouse Ave. Now, this meeting was supposed to take place between men of rational thinking. This meeting between me and the tough dwarfs... Sailor Kid, Douglas Boy, and Brat Worst... was hopefully a guarantee for rational thinking to take place, I thought. Yes, so I thought when I now arrived to Kidstone Airport... now at Kidstone Airport, taking a taxi to that hotel, waiting Hearts. When I arrived and finally understood that this meeting of "rational male thinking" also really should take place without much ado and objections... when I finally understood that, then I also understood that I could count on that the three very tough dwarfs should begin to be more involved in serious discussions about industrial espionage.

Yes, and it so appeared when those tough dwarfs arrived. They were quite involved... but just as the intellectual level of this discussion was on its peak... then those tall Wifes of those tough dwarfs showed up and demanded that their husbands shouldn't sign on for any dangerous agent mission. The tall Wifes of the small men did hold me in contempt. Not funny.

I now blew the trumpet and all men in the room put their scout hats on, shouting: 'I am prepared!'

When these women realized how tough we men were, then they just passed off. Women!! We men, however, did stay cool and we fixed ourselves some meatballs for dinner. Some meatballs were also ready-prepared in the freezer. Now, I did for some inscrutable reason identify me, myself, and I with three meatballs in the freezer.

I then, at dinner-time, turned towards my short work-mates and between some hungry bites, I said: 'As a matter of fact, I now happen to have him shadowed, that German fellow named Reiner Beck being employed at "my" Cupboard Department. This Mr. Beck who has specialized in economics of transportation- techniques and who did evaluate possible such techniques and related to "transportation-problems like transportation-problems of dangerous goods". I have considered Mr. Beck's profile of competence. Now, having this competence of Mr. Beck in mind; I have been written down this Reiner Beck's list of companies... like manufacturers of explosives, manufacturers of long-distance trucks, building companies, haulage contractors, etc. Hm, that Mr. Beck had also listed some mysterious people... for instance a Swedish businessman called Mr. Hallert, a fellow which I could locate to Hannover or was it Henover.'

Sailor Kid, Douglas Roy, and Brat Worst now mumbled something which ended up in some questions of how they should enter this awful criminal Swedish game... as agents, working for DBIA. There were some loud voices.

I was very controlled when I answered, somewhat shouting: 'Gentlemen! Order, You have to play it cool if you are going to work and participate as agents in this serious, dangerous, criminal international game now going on! Now, let me finish, and let me get to the point. Now, here is a travel-list to some countries... and listed for travels are some people at that BAD Cupboard Department "of mine". For instance, listed for travels is... a young candidate called Maria Headwall who is going to red Yugoslavia. Another young candidate who is called Akin Sellin is going to Kenya, Amjed Babar is that candidate from Egypt, Akin Burglos is going to Italy, Hassan is a candidate from Iran who is going to go to or who is going to communicate with his home country. Etc. Yes, I just mentioned some few BAD people who have done some traveling... and when people make a journey, then things might happen... I think or just guess that Hassan and Amjed might operate throw some fire cross-circle. Some relay race perhaps. Now, Sailor Kid, Douglas Boy, and Brat Worst,... do you want to help me in my reconnaissance work which will relate to what I just now have told you, do you?'

Sailor Kid, Douglas Boy, and Brat Worst nodded, and that meant... that this plan of limited reconnaissance-work which I had put before them... this plan was now accepted. The three short men also promised to take care of Roy Carson who always was chased by some Swedish taxman. Maybe, Roy Carson was under suspicion... or otherwise, the Swedish taxmen just followed theirtrue nature.

Chapter 2
FIELD STUDIES

Back in Stockholm, in some toilet or lavatory being related to some pizza-bar being named "The Golden Bullet", there I now met Mirrony Stuntman... Mirrony Stuntman who now slipped out of my Jones-identity, and I myself now had slipped out of my Jones-identity and slipped into my old genuine identity as Noman Skeleton - and when those activities were over and done with, then I went back to BAD-Department being "my" Cupboard Department. Yes, I was back at "my" Cupboard Department... where time just in accordance with a certain agreement, a medical consultant from that pharmaceutical company Astra AB. Yes, I did... and that name was Paavo Waltzer... and we had agreed upon a meeting in the library, at the Monte Fresco University. We discussed lead-time and costs for medicals related to that company called Astra. This company was a fairly good representative of the pharmaceutical industry according to Paavo Waltzer who perhaps was biased since he was one of Astra's pharmaceutical consultants. I, after some time excused myself and phoned my dwarf-friend Brat Worst. I told him to be around as soon as possible.

This fellow Paavo Waltzer now mentioned something about social accounting, probably related to marketing and over-consumption of medicals. We then discussed stocks in trade... of medicals, and medical statistics, and how we had solved some simple problem of a certain simple econometric problem. Yes, economical problems.

Time passed, and I looked at my high-quality wrist-watch. Finally, I told myself, that by now my dwarf-friend Brat Worst must have finished his work at the parking-lot. Yes, so I thought, looking out of the window... while Paavo Waltzer went through some figures of medical trade, figures he had got from AstraAB.

Paavo Waltzer then delivered our "report" to senior lecturer Boo Sellstedt... something which I let him do, alone. I had done the work, anyhow – except for the figures from AstraAB which I had got from Paavo Waltzer probably felt he had some other more important things to take care of at AstraAB. He was probably right and I wasn't exactly overloaded with work. Gosh! In this very moment I went to the toilets where I should find my strange so called "twin-brother" Mirrony Stuntman, according to some agreement of ours.

Yes, I now found my so-called "twin-brother" who now was dressed, not in his old clothes as Mirrony Stuntman... but as any Mr. Jones, or was it Mr. Smith? I looked at Mirrony and said: 'I think that chap from Astra being named Paavo Waltzer... wants to get in touch with all those professors and auditors at "my" strange BAD Cupboard Department.'

I paused and made a gesture in the direction towards "my" Strange Cupboard Department, and then I added: That's because Astra wants to increase its good-will. Those Astra-people want a good consumer-profile, and for that reason, Paavo Waltzer have in mind some kind of social accounting. Haw-haw-haw, it sounds to me like some kind of advertising or public relations, although he claims he is doing some scientific thesis or theses. I am just a little bit suspicious that those great flags of social responsibility should be related to some dubious social accounting... which is supposed to be scientific... I instead suspect that this idea, which originated from AstraAB, is just another way of hiding some shandy business... showing the good deeds in some public social accounting and hiding the bad deeds in some secret internal accounting. Hm, access to some hostage like pawn - and internal accounting." I and Mirrony now went into an empty class-room where we both changed clothes and identity. I was a man in disguise again. I was alias Mr. Jones covering for 027 Dodger Warner and Mirrony Ston.

Through the window I now could see how this kid-looking dwarf Brat Worst did pretend to "play" in the parking-lot. He had mounted and now he just checked some secret transponder plus that also secret drive-writer being likewise mounted and checked; a secret drive-writer which could register the geographic movements of a certain car during each car-ride.

I said: 'Look! Now, this Paavo Waltzer is going towards the parking-lot, and now he starts his car. The very same car. Which Brat Worst has "played" with. I will follow this Paavo Waltzer. I'll use that car you rented, when you pretended to be a certain Mr. Jones... dear Mirrony. So long Mirrony Stuntman alias Norman Skeleton... since Brat Worst is waiting at that car you rented.'

Yes, Brat Worst was waiting for me. We two, did now shadow Paavo Waltzer, and we soon found out that this fellow Waltzer was driving to "The South Hospital", where he stopped his car. We then very discreetly followed or shadowed this Paavo Waltzer through the corridors. Brat Worst went first and I followed after. Yes! Paavo went to this Dr HerCo-Witch at MAD-Clinic.

Hmm, Paavo Waltzer probably reported about my present state of mood for his "friend" Dr HerCo-Witch. The same Dr HerCo-Witch who wrote my diagnosis. Hm, based on what kind of investigation? Who knows, perhaps this Dr HerCO-Witch could alter my diagnosis... if Paavo Waltzer and other people representing the pharmaceutical industry called for such a change... to alter my diagnosis! Hm, I could see Paavo Waltzer and Dr HerCo-Witch discussing... behind a pane of glass. Gee, I got a creepy feeling that there was a suspect blood-testing undead creature of no moral... from Roumania... around. Oh, and so-called noble people from the big Swedish pharmaceutical company Astra needed some partners. Hm, the public sector and the private sector working together and it takes two people to do some bloody waltzing. Well, I now still looked at those two people, Dr HerCo-Witch and Paavo Waltzer. Gee, Vikings from the private sector needed vampires from the public sector, and I was the victim! Hm, but I sure didn't want to stay in the victim-position!

Anyway, I now more than strongly suspected that these two "gentlemen of dark nature", Waltzer and Dr HerCo-Witch, took part in a certain Swedish plot of consensus involving criminal co-operation... obviously first of all between one organization in the public sector, like "The South Hospital" and MAD-Clinic, and another organization in the private sector, like the pharmaceutical company AstraAB. Yes, some criminal line of relations and the medical consultant and candidate for the doctorate Paavo Waltzer was some awful human link... a criminal cooperation which also had the criminal purpose to twist around some concepts in that diagnosis of mine!

Yes, and this had something to do with this blacklisting leading to extortion... where I, Noman Skeleton, was put in some kind of hostage like situation and also therefore put on probation... so I believed. Yes, and of course BAD-Department being part of Monte Fresco University and Mad-Clinic being part of The South Hospital and also other organizations like that one of private enterprise named AstraAB... were part of this cooperation of criminal consensus. I made a face of distaste. I then did my conclusions and I now know how well-organized the Swedish works of blacklisting and extortion and experimental tests really were and now still are and these must be the true facts. Well, observation and empiric data. I now did hurry to the laundry of The South Hospital, Where I in a hurry exchanged coded blinking looks with Donna Sickolina, a friend of Yoke and Strudel. Yes, and according to that code of blinking looks... Donna Sickolina should meet me at a certain slot machine. Unnoticeable... we, I and Donna Sickolina, arranged a meeting outside a bread-coffee slot-machine... at the big entry hall of The South Hospital.

Donna Sickolina worked sometimes at the laundry and sometimes at the ambulant library at The South Hospital, I was told. She now also told me she just had been around in that MAD-Clinic as an ambulating librarian. On the sly she found out about certain diagnoses; diagnoses made by Dr HerCo-Witch. Donna now mentioned that she had observed that there sometimes were mysterious ways of making a diagnosis up to date at that MAD-Clinic, especially as far as a certain patient named Noman Skeleton... was concerned.

Donna Sickolina whispered: 'Those doctors working at this MAD-Clinic will bring up that Skeleton diagnosis for discussions at certain points of time... and those points of time are always connected to those very budget occasions at MAD-Clinic. Now, I could of course have mistaken your Skeleton-diagnosis for that Skeleton diagnosis of Basil Addams being patient and an American struggling painter who had been put in the isolation freezer of MAD-Clinic... despite all wild protests coming from his girlfriend who had offered to take care of her boyfriend why was this so impossible? Hm, MAD-Clinic and ulterior motives. For some odd reason there always then also was some waltzing pharmaceutical consultant around..." I in a philosophical way said: 'Yes, who wanted to stress the confiding but also criminal cooperation between a certain Swedish public sector and a certain Swedish private sector. My guess is that one such fellow is that pharmaceutical consultant who is named Paavo Waltzer and if so, then he no doubt is around when budget matters are to be discussed. Paavo Waltzer is then later also around because he is the man who should order how to alter this and that Skeleton diagnosis... and any such dubious "order of a diagnosis" is a matter for negotiations where you also consider political and economic aspects like the budgetary proceeding... and then some people pay more attention to economic aspects and also to political aspects than to some kind of decent medical care and therapy and work-therapy which follows from the true diagnosis?!

Yes, truth isn't always beautiful, but if you bend the truth by "ordering some slide on the indicators resulting in some diagnosis"... then this bent truth may turn out to be very profitable in certain cases, and hereby the budgetary –process is of some interest. Yes, the patient may die or at least get his life destroyed... but if it is in the profitable National Interest then so be it. Yes, and then one has to do some waltzing with the truth, as some Mathilda may say in Australia.' Donna Sickolina:

'Oh, terrible things really do happen in this wicked world.'

Suddenly, I could see Paavo Waltzer in this big entry hall of The South Hospital followed or tailed by a very discreet Brat Worst. Paavo Waltzer was now leaving The South Hospital as he went to his car in the parking lot.

I now at once said bye-bye to Donna Sickolina... and then I joined Brat Worst. Yes, I and Brat, we both now continued to follow this Paavo Waltzer, and somewhat later I and Brat found out that this Paavo Waltzer now was driving to some premises of SPRI, SPRI which can be read as the Swedish State Planning Rationalization Institute.

I stated and asked: "Well,... Brat. Now, we are outside SPRI, where a certain Steve Hobbard works. Steve Hobbard from BAD-Department. I just wonder what kind of guys Paavo Waltzer now will visit?" Brat Worst: 'A matter of guesswork, but I should bet some money on Steve Hobbard.' I asked: "You mounted one or two transponders on other cars as well, didn't you?"

Brat Worst showed me some gadgets saying: "Yes, those transponders will be activated only when a transmitter like this is sending and then whether the car is moving or not. Then the hidden drive-writer will first electronically memorize the car's position in the center of a circle and the car movements... and then simultaneously while the car driving is going on or then later when this electronic memory is read and displayed... one can watch a circle and two axes of coordinators... Yes, those movements of the car can be watched on a computer screen or be printed out on a sheet of paper or both.

Time and date are also printed down in an automatic fashion. Now, while the car is moving... then at the same time a secret transmitter can be sending - tailing signals due to a transponder on the car being tailed. It's all some work of skillful programming. I and Brat Worst did now use our big old fashion car-phone calling this second dwarf-assistant, Douglas Boy... who was staying in the neighborhood. Now, the car-phone apparatus in the two cars involved in this communication circus of the air... had both a coder and decoder which hopefully should make a traditional police radio useless.

Douglas Boy now agreed on or suggested - that he now, after our phone conversation, should go to The South Hospital in order to shadow... not Paavo Waltzer, now being at the SPRI-house, but that MAD-Clinic in The South Hospital... Douglas Boy who now could use a transmitter in his own car and then a transponder plus a drive-writer which he should mount on that car of Dr. HerCo-Witch, while waiting for Dr HerCo-Witch... to end his day at MAD-Clinic.

I and Brat Worst waited for something to happen at that SPRI building, and we waited for a few hours, but nothing happened... and instead, I got a new phone call from Douglas Boy. I asked if this Douglas Boy had some information for us, me and Brat Worst? Then or now this Douglas Boy told us that he had done what he was supposed to do,… and then the phone conversation was over.

I and Brat Worst continued to wait for something to happen at that SPRI house, and we waited for a few hours more, but nothing happened and instead, I got a new phone call from Douglas Boy... and a phone conversation took place between me and Douglas Boy. Douglas Boy now told me that he had been tailing this Dr HerCo-Witch and his big car while Douglas Boy himself was using a small pedal car with that so called new pedal engine,... and all the way this driving and tailing took place until Dr HerCo-Witch arrived to Monte Fresco University. There were some parking activities. Then, still tailing this Dr HerCo-Witch... through the corridors of Monte Fresco University... this Douglas Boy could see how Dr HerCo-Witch vanished into some room... and that room was situated at the Department of Pedagogy at Monte Fresco University, I now was told...

Yes, Douglas Boy now told me so, and he also told me that this Dr HeCo-Witch had arrived a little bit too early so far a while this meeting room was empty and then Douglas sneaked in... and he placed some bugs... and then the men for the meeting concerned arrived... but then Douglas Boy just could start his record player and vanish into his own plastic bag in the very same room. Now, the conversation could be and was recorded due to three bugs and a record player. Yes, and then Douglas Boy also in person being present could overhear the conversation going on it that room at the Department of Pedagogy...

After an hour or so the conversation come to an end... and other people should enter the room, and in that crowdy situation, then Douglas Boy in a speedy and also discreet invisible way succeeded to lay hands on his bugs and record player which now had recorded a certain conversation between Dr. HerCo-Witch, Dr. Edfield and Dr. Stockfeldt. Still being in telecommunications this Douglas Boy told me that those people, Dr HeCo-Witch and Dr Edfield and Dr Stockfeldt, they were all interested in psycho-social tests and how to develop measurement, instruments, and alarms related to internal conditions inside the body and brain. Basically, their interest was concentrated to the endocrine system and the nervous system,… that this Douglas Boy now had found out over hearing the recalled conversation through that recorder device. Hm,… these men named HerCo-Witch and Dr. Edfield and Dr. Stockfeldt were also interested in those new product developments and product developments of instruments,… often electronic instruments used in hospital care like surgical operations, childbirth, and the like.

Those instruments which in different ways could participate in medical therapy and/or diagnoses. Yes, and all this interesting talk was now also recalled and overheard by me and Brat due to this small fellow Douglas Boy or at least some seemingly harmless parts of the talking, being however coded when entering into and being in the medium of air. Hm, we had a code of communication which was impossible to break. Now, Douglas Boy told me through telecommunications, that all that product level development and all this new product development, which often involved electronic solutions, was the very reason why some more genuine meeting between some dubious fellows should take place... and at least Dr. HerCo-Wtich should attend this second such meeting. Now, this first meeting just attended was obviously still not finished, and therefore... Douglas Boy now once again had to do some shadowing of Dr. HeCo-

Witch and his big car. Yes, some shadowing where Douglas Boy was using a small pedal car which also was using some mopped engine, especially practical in the traffic jams... and thanks to that big coded car phone apparatus of Douglas Boy... I and Brat Worst could now listen to Douglas Boy who still was tailing Dr HerCo-Witch and his big car... being stuck in a traffic jam. Yes, due to telecommunications we could join Douglas Boy... some time passed.

Finally, Dr HerCo-Witch arrived to SPRI where he obviously should meet not only Steve Hobbard and Paavo Waltzer... but also some other people now arriving like Dr. Nichols and Dr. Mabon, and Dr. Stockfeldt, and Dr. Edfield. Steve Hobbard was perhaps some formal host representing SPRI and some university all those people just mentioned plus that politico-boss for SPRI named Leni N Beginman came out of the so-called SPRI building and now they together obviously should go to somewhere. Hm, probably this awful woman or rather witch named Leni N Beginman was behind this informal meeting of talks. Hm, patterns of communication in some elite-sphere. Yes, hm... and now this gang of people went to STU which is a Swedish abridgment for the "The Board of Technological Progress", where the Swedish word Styrelse Board and the Swedish word Teknisk Technological and the Swedish word Utveckling Progress/Development - will give the abridgment STU. Ye STU. Hm, interesting!

Those "gentlemen of dark nature" had all studied instruments and medicals - being related to internal conditions inside the nervous system and inside the endocrine system - and more than one such process may be dangerous... Therefore, we need different new instruments and improved instruments, often based on micro-electronics and nano-mechanics - and so I thought. Dr Nichols was here of interest, being a member of STU. Hm, after some time I, and Brat now could see some people in a momentum of leaving the STU building... a momentum which suddenly was lost and freezed due to discussions where only lips were moving.

Brat Worst did now after this STU meeting, do some lip reading – thanks to the strongest binoculars in the world which also could be part of a movie camera. Yes... and after that lip reading and when that leaving of the STU building gained momentum... Brat Worst now started to tail Dr Mabon, Hunter Mabon. I, being a part of that car tailing, sometimes released Brat Worst at the wheel... "perhaps?" In my capacity as alias Mr. Jones. Dr Mabon stopped at some premises being named or shortened SPI. Dr Mabon went inside this SPI building and after a while he appeared on some balcony high-up in a VonOben position.

This Mabon now talked to some staff managers like Roll Hamson representing the staff management of BAD department or Cupboard Department and Hardy Viceman representing the staff management of this whole Monte Fresco University... and Dr Mabon did even some talking with that high executive and high ranking director general representing ... SPI=State Personal Institute, and that director general was named Stringon Pullman... Gee, there was also to be found that woman up there in a balcony position named Leni N Beginman, being that boss or director general of SPRI=State Planning Rationalization Institute Yes, I could now see those five people who all somehow were linked to scientific staff management,

I could see those five people now standing on a balcony talking, while they in some silly car accident adding to the demand of hospital care and work therapy.

Yes, and now Brat did some filming from one of our cars and then I did some developing work related to those first and second and third rolls of film, and the last roll of the film ended with the depopulation of a certain balcony. Hm, where had I read something about that new product development of digital cameras should make things more easy? Anyway, I and Brat now looked at the rolls of film just being developed. We could read the lips of those dubious fellows. Lips telling us that Roll Hamson and Hardy Viceman and Stringon Pullman... all men of some practical scientific staff management... were in agreement with Dr Hunter Mabon to get in touch with Dr Stockfeldt and Dr Edfield at the Department of Pedagogy. Now, this politico-woman being Director-General Leni N Beginman seemed to agree. Hmm, there was also some talk about something which was called... "The Secret Department of Black Pedagogy". Hm, still sitting in some kind of car... I did some thinking. Hm, was it possible that something illegal was going on around the very Department of Pedagogy?

Was it possible that the people there at the Department of Pedagogy were familiar with and even had their ways of how to practice and apply the art of black pedagogy, in some informal way. Hm, like Dr Stockfeldt and Dr Edfield. Yes,… and therefore when this black pedagogy was exercised at BAD Cupboard Department... then Dr Mabon and others like Dr Stockfeldt and Dr Edfield did see to it that I was the one... who was subject to a sick experiment related to staff management and to black pedagogy...

Yes, I now realized that, and on top of everything... this Dr HerCo-Witch who represented the expert knowledge regarding certain medicals related to neuro-physiology and endocrinology. Some possible medical therapy was obviously or could obviously also in some extreme situations be connected to a very hard black pedagogy! Oh, as a terrified human laboratory mouse... I had to avoid those medical pills!

Later, at BAD Department, my so-called "strange twin or double being named Mirrony Stuntman and also me... we were both collecting information about that Astra consultant Paavo Waltzer and Dr HerCo-Witch and the same goes for that fellow from Egypt named Amjed Babar and his compatriot Mrs Mohga Badran... staying at the Egypt embassy... and hopefully did we also collect information about that Candidate Zabrodsky from red Czechoslovakia and also that Candidate Hassan from Iran and also that BAD Br Nichols and also that Guran Edby being some kind of EDP specialist like Dr Nichols and that BAD Mr Beck studying tricky dangerous transportation, and why should we no forget to map Dr Stoclfeldt and Dr Edfield from that dubious department of Pedagogy. Hm, some MAD Dr HerCo-Witch and his suspect partner Paavo Waltzer from AstraCompany. Yes, people have to be mapped! Sure, and BAD Department was obviously a place where different people met and exchanged information also about black pedagogy. Hm, Mirrony and me... we did some shadowing and we did some checking and we found some indications of experiments in black pedagogy, being included in scientific staff management!

I and Mirrony did all this, sometimes together. Hmm, I now began to see some pattern of relations around BAD Cupboard Department... coming – of which some no doubt were criminal and some were double and some were part of a dubious network and some didn't work as they should. Hm, I was now late in the evening trying to collect additional information in that room next to mine... that room of Mrs Lawdotted from the faculty of law.

When I was finished in that room of Mrs Lawdotted I intended to visit the room of Mr Presstone from The Media Research Centre, and I almost lost my ability to breathe. A ghost appeared in some fancy uniform and I noticed his white gloves.

I exclaimed: "Oh, what an elegant and chic ghost, appearing... while I am complaining of, about or over my psycho-social existential situation - a situation of psycho-torture and humiliation and experiments in black pedagogy here at BAD-Department." I asked: "Who are you?"

The Elegant Ghost: "I am a learned man of science who works at a concentration camp at a small rot schwarz weiss German town named Auschwitz. I asked: "Doing what?" The Elegant Ghost: 'I design performances when it comes to medical and also social and also psycho-social experiments with human beings involving also black pedagogy.' I asked: 'Do a BAD and MAD fellow ghost like you have a name?' The Elegant Ghost: "Dr Mengele."

Dr Mengele now added: 'I also know about your name being Noman Skeleton and in addition to that I know about your situation... Hm, an interesting situation involving also those BAD people at BAD

Department. I want to compare those your Swedish BAD University officers with my German SS officers of the University education... regarding attitudes.'

I said: "Yes, it's interesting to watch that Swedish and German attitude thing and to see how superior academic people treat UnterMenchen like handicapped people like me being an Helge-elk and Jews being swine... and KKK are hunting and hanging monkies=negroes. Yes, some people have animal status in Sweden, German, and USA. Hm, negroes and apartheid laws like Nürnberg laws in USA."

Dr Mengele: 'Yes, you can transport those kinds of people or I mean goods to some place,... Hm, it's funny – nowadays they talk about delivering the living goods of prostitution.'

I remarked: "Well, fill me in on how BAD people talk about different categories of people who they could deliver, me included... and how I shall fit in... in this sex trade and the sex industry." Dr Mengele: "Sure, UnterMench... and until I have found that out - auf wiedersehen." The Ghost disappeared and I was in the solitude, again. However, now... a new ghost appeared the ghost of Abraham Lincoln! The Ghost of Abraham Lincoln: "I overheard you and this German fellow Dr Mengele. Now, I don't like the slave trade and slavery and BAD people. Now, I'll go, but I'll be back.

I'll keep an eye on you. I'll see you around."

Now, also this ghost disappeared in a flickering way and I began gradually to be in the solitude, again. Yes, in this BAD university-corredor. Hm, Abraham Lincoln seemed to care about me and my situation and my right to prove myself and in that respect he=Abraham was an alright fellow. Old Abe didn't like slave-like situations, and therefore he expected me to liberate myself... even if I was helped by my mother with food and lodgings. Well, Old Abe had a wife who helped him a lot in his career... he understood that behind a great man, there was always at least one fine woman.

Chapter 3

A MEETING ABOUT FIELD STUDIES,

where I was some kind of rapporteur

I was dressed like an artist when I now installed myself as the very secret agent... 027 Dodger Warner. I was installed in my secret spy centre at Solid Star Street, in Stockholm, where especially to be found was that very big library. I was in that big library room surrounded by bookshelves and books. A library which obviously was not yet replaced by some home computer or PC and a number of discs. Hm, it might be stupid to store secrets on a PC... I am not sure about this but I'll find out. I now looked at two photos while waiting for that stand-in for the big DBIA boss, Mr. Z. One photo showed my "old" acquaintance Web Spooky and he was that stand-in for the big DBIA boss, Mr. Z. Yes, and he should and could now finally be accompanied by this chartered accountant named X-ray Charlie, and there was a photo of him too. I now expected those two fellows to show up any minute. I did not mind this meeting for I had worked alone in this library for many weeks now. When Web Spooky and X-ray Charlie finally entered "my" secret spy centre, then I noticed they were accompanied by Ramon Freud, Brat Worst, and Hunt Recardo.

There I stood... all dressed up as an artist as if I was working under the ridges in Paris... and moreover... I now also had the nerve to show how I was trying to create three mystery paintings was focusing on a Christmas tree decorated with dolls. A man stood beside that Christmas tree and investigated if two dolls of different materials should fall with different or equal speeds down to the floor. The second mystery painting was also focusing on this Christmas tree. Another man stood behind or beside that Christmas tree. A third man stood behind that Christmas tree and studied how doll price was falling. Dolls were usually the most expensive when they were fresh! Yes, and then there was only one way downward!

For some reason no one was interested in my paintings. Odd! Maybe some powerful interests in the slave trade... wanted to stop me.

I asked: 'Spooky why have you brought X-Ray Charlie to "my" place at Solid Star Street? I mean we two are both working for this private agency, for "The Dealogram Business Intelligence Agency"... but is this agency really of some concern to this man, X-Ray Charlie? Do you X-Ray have any letter of attorney?' Now X-Ray showed what he had got, a letter of attorney to issue special warrants of arrest signed by FBI and CIA... plus special control charters to check Swedish companies and non-Swedish companies in Sweden, and Swedish authorities and Swedish citizens and non-Swedish citizens in Sweden.

I said: "I can see that this X-Ray Charlie has brought two documents with him. A charter to check Swedes and a special warrant of attorney from the Federal Government to authorize arrests. Yes, and some special control charter plus this special warrant of attorney can be used to check also our Business. Intelligence, the agency, DBIA... while being around in Sweden. Always... some guy from the central bureaucracy who thinks that every private agent is some kind of baby in shorts who can't run his own affairs!''

X-Ray Charlie now said: ''You are not necessarily so, unable... but let me put it this way... You need in certain situations doing certain work tasks... you then may need someone who looks at your doings just one time or maybe twice just to check on you during all that time you are writing all those books and then you need some small hints. Hm, and then praxis has had it that you have got a few right hints and some more wrong hints plus a lot of unnecessary hints telling you what you already knew. Now, I have got those charters from the Swedes to check the Swedes... and the reason why I have got those charters from the Swedes is... because otherwise, the Swedes will find themselves in an even more uncomfortable situation.

Yes, but I won't tell anybody anything about my findings as long as a certain hostage-like situation does last and also as long as if you Noman, and/or your Mirrony should have started writing books about this criminal situation, but still not haven't finished writing an assumption will come true and this predicted book writing continues... then it's important to have in mind that should you fail in this writing of your books... then I will never be able to go public with my findings of auditing.''

I said: ''You really put your words very nicely. I being an independent soul, now realize that I as Mirrony I am forced to send hints into some media buzz within a framework of cooperation... on this early stage, even.''

Hunt Recardo: ''Yes, we need to know where you or I mean Mirrony know where you stand and you need to believe to know where we stand... and your mother's apartment is already bugged... but I do not know about your small house. However, at BAD Department there are BAD bugs."

Web Spooky: 'We, I and DBIA and FBI and CIA and X-Ray Charlie, we now want you 027 to solve that hostage-like Skeleton problem before X-ray Charlie enters the scene.'

I replied: 'Well, this sounds difficult, and I can't give you more than half a promise. I mean that I think I can solve that hostage-like Skeleton problem before X-Ray has left the scene. What I then need is a whole promise that... if you want information from me, then you will also pay for it.' Web Spooky: 'Oh, this is something we always have tried to avoid. What about if you need information from us, will you pay for it?'

I answered: 'Well, if you can spare me, then you won't have to pay me. Nowadays, however, the secret police in Sweden or Swedish intelligence isn't as open as it once used to be or was supposed to be. Still, maybe both FBI, and CIA, and DBIA can spare me?'

Web Spooky: 'Well, a strange individual like you 027 Dodger Warner... is no doubt in this situation for us quite irreplaceable. I know, Anyway, before you... 027 Dodger Warner... will get fat paychecks I want you to develop certain hypotheses regarding this Skeleton problem.'

I... who in this spy business always was remembering, that I always could and sometimes should speak about myself as if I was a third person... I now answered: 'Yes, problems and hypotheses. That fellow

Skeleton... he has been caught in a web of spooky expert decisions and expert statements and expert doings always going on behind his back and which he, therefore, doesn't know anything about, Web Spooky... and those expert decisions and those expert doings and expert statements, which were taken above Noman's ignorant head, have probably and mostly been focusing on, specialized on... how to control human beings. Yes, Noman Skeleton is a fellow...' and now I pointed at myself saying: '... who obviously needs to be controlled - according for the experts, but not according to me.

Well, but since there is a wager situation then control of me=Skeleton is necessary. I paused and added: "I would say that this strange web of spooky expert-related decisions and exper-related doings and expert-related statements being taken behind Noman's back by BAD university people at BAD Department... is influenced by representatives from unions, organized private companies, the bureaucratic nomenclature... and those Swedish often corporative related people have in a cruel and awful way stopped this or that research going on or meant to be started up at this or that scientific institution and many a research project being stopped has been stopped since it has become inconvenient or is linked to this my Noman case at BAD Department. Yes, some Swedish less visible KKK fascists who do hide behind kkk hoods and who in this hidden state of things in a criminal expert writing/reporting way represent the Swedish organized so-called natural interests which man delayed or stopped Noman's "research for in some way disabled people".

Yes, the so-called Swedish natural interests are being integrated in the Swedish state apparatus... these natural interests have very keen ears when it comes to wanted and not wanted research, and when it comes to cases Scorpio we have some Swedish research and criminal opportunities! Yes, and with criminal opportunities will come ulterior motives! Sure, those now in certain circles have notorious Swedish ulterior motives!' Web Spooky: "Yes, and because of all this a criminal BAD research program at BAD Department being much Council were meant to compromise Noman Skeleton."

I said: "Now, where here we can see how that Swedish corporative-related bureaucratic nomenclature is influencing the people at BAD Department to be exercising some very hard black pedagogy where also The Department of Pedagogy at Monte Fresco University has involved thanks to some additional budget means... some very hard black pedagogy with ulterior motives/influences... and thus here we can see how that Swedish corporative related bureaucratic nomenclature, being skillful in coordination do nothing less than using very brutal and cynical scientific methods of human staff management and human control. Truth... is horrible... and therefore taboo!" I in bitter words also said: "Yes, black pedagogy being related to scientific methods of kicking down and bending down and humiliating people with the purpose of human control.

The individual being named Noman Skeleton has to be or has to become, an if necessary blind, disinformed, obedient tool for the Swedish Corporative Welfare State and its hidden criminal purpose! Yes, criminal black BAD staff management by Roland Hanson of Roll Hamson who also said... "One should put a knife in him where him was me=Noman Skeleton. Hm, my employment is some embezzlement of let's say $50,000. Gee, some amazing Swedish solidarity!!!

Web Spooky: 'Hm, interesting. And that Professor Person and his colleague Professor Sunway Sweetiepie didn't tell you anything!

I replied: 'No! Hm, some first questions! Well, I don't know if those professors were in full control of this game around me, but what I do know is that they kept silent! Moreover, what I also know is that I have been exposed to cruel staff management sabotage... for some strange reason!'

Web Spooky: 'Oh! How interesting! Those professors more than just knew something about what was going on and they didn't tell you anything. Now, can you tell me more about this staff management sabotage going on?'

I answered: "Yes, of course. Now, I regard this staff-management sabotage as a case study of a staff-management sabotage where there has been and is an evil ring of people and organizations involved pulling the strings around Mr Skeleton. Yes, we have here certain evil forces of collective and individual decisions taken, self-interests which aren't particularely interested to obey Swedish laws and decisions of work-therapy, not at all! Some faceless people of thos corporative Swedish power-structure around BAD Department do not have an interest to help Noman Skeleton, but instead they all have a common criminal interest to indoctrinate this bone-like soul of Skeleton into helplessness! It's obvious that there is a common interest to try to offer Skeleton a break dance? Dance Macabre! Peadagogy of fear?

Those invisible crooks in the corridors of power, they want to break me! Yes, and it is obviously funny to hurt me and destroy my reputation and destroy my whole life without being seen, and without taking responsibility for evil-doings like most citizens have to do. They use Roll Hamson of Roland Hamson as a criminal tool. Yes, and Swedish media-people do here act like spineless hench men which Mr Presstone from The Media Research Department can observe and then he can also ask Carrol Foge from Wasp Express... An ugly gossip-like media-circus of column through allusions will develop and all the time this Mrs Lawdotted from the faculty of Law... is around BAD-Department next door to me, for some purpose... whatever that purpose could be. Well, spineless henchmen who nevertheless want to be important actors or an important collective actor... Mumm, Swedish so-called individual actors, but they are in reality part of this and that Swedish collective actor."

Web Spooky: "Well, and then when it comes to mostly gang up with World-Communism and World-terrorism, but in some situations, they can also play off Soviet against the USA... and therefore you can't reduce these calculating Swedes to just henchmen... to either side of "The Cold Global InterContinental World-War No, the Swedes their own driving in some own line of traffic... and their cronies are driving fast in a beige Volvo Coupe."

I replied and said: "Well-well-well, Swedes and friends of Swedes have got access to keys to cars, cars which they are driving too fast and because of this I am some kind of hostage-like pawn in a certain game of extortion and this has made me walk right into a Swedish environment blacklisted of fear and godless crime... I feel that it is now almost ridiculous to talk about that responsibility for results and costs... as far as that relief-work and therapy-work of quicksand regarding Skeleton is concerned, or as a first question is it not? Hmm, that responsibility for results and costs must have vanished into thin air/bribe-air due to side-motives or ulterior motives... related to criminal corporative politics=power and crime-related business of much money and many job opportunities. Hm, that was both a question and answer."

I added: "Hmm, in Sweden fine laws and decisions are taken and then broken... and the victim who claims that his rights are offended... he is declared; persona non grata! How was all this possible without an open conflict and alarm pulling... especially since people of law and media were very present... around BAD-Department... when it comes to office rooms next door... Ugh, that is a second question! Ugh, that red or rouge Swedish ugly distorted democracy still staying beige!" I now looked at Brat Worst, Hunt Recardo, X-Ray Charlie, Ramon Freud and Web Spooky... hitting my forehead, before I went on saying: "Now, out there you can find Swedish souls of ignorant contempt, as far as work therapy and research are concerned... and there is nothing funny when a fellow like me is asking questions about guidelines regarding decisions about objectives, techniques, measures, methods when it comes to work therapy!

There has to be some methodology for dealing with any reduced functional ability... related to human organisms! This shouldn't be a taboo, especially when I and some people like me who suffer from small functional problems and unemployment need to defend ourselves against the so-called normal population and their neglect to observe the laws and decisions taken and their evil minds being willing to stamp and stigmatize us, feeling superior. Nevertheless, I guess some few people at BAD-Department who wanted to give me their support were threatened to become stamped and to become stigmatized! Yes, and I was left alone and some of my brothers of functional misfortune were also left alone as human organisms inside social organizations and there working poorly not being helped by some scientific staff management according to a social charter! Yes, that is how things should not be, but nevertheless were and are! Hmm, I wanted things to be... otherwise according to a social charter at least if a nation=society has reached a certain economic level and become the so-called affluent society where people have got tired of material values and want to recognize working life."

Hunt Recardo: "Well, since this recognition of working life hasn't been taken seriously where it has taken place... then this by me the methodology for dealing with reduced human functional abilities was non-existing, meaning that there was not even, humbug talk minding ulterior motives, I strongly suppose... but could all this be an experiment? I let that third question hang in the air for a while, and then I finally said: "Well, in my case as far as I can see there was in the first place not any decent methodology at all... instead I was deliberately exposed to psycho-social torture as if this was some kind of work therapy... work therapy was sometimes however also at best just decoration... and that is some hypothesis of mine. Secondly, as far as work therapy and research are concerned we must rise the question... are decisions of work therapy and research education registered? Who has taken those decisions? There's always somebody that will see to it that decisions are taken or not taken... and who is responsible for taking certain decisions and then executing them or for avoiding taking necessary decisions. What's the purpose of a decision or an obvious non-decision? Is, that purpose registered? Signatures? Gee, some lack of goodwill and ulterior motives! No incentives... or ulterior negative and maybe private incentives some setting for an experiment.

Brat Worst" 'Oh, permit a small dwarf to ask if not everybody will understand that people being employed at BAD-Department have been quite careless? Maybe this is so... deliberately! I continued angry and depressed but still controlled bumblebee when I said: 'Definitely.... deliberately, or at least we have to work therapy and research were not carried out... and why Noman wasn't offered any explanation! Who is responsible for some execution of decisions... and who is responsible for some explanation if non-execution of decisions?' Hunt Recardo: 'Yes, that fourth question being a double question was also a good question!'

Now I rose my forefinger and said: 'Fifth question... the follow-up of this Noman-like work therapy, and the auditing of such activities should be but isn't performed by Lee SaLasso once employed by BAD-Department, but now employed by "The National Sweish Audit Office". The fifth question now asks if Lee SaLasso or his colleagues in public auditing at all check measures and accounts being used related to work therapy at BAD-Department; or has he or have his colleagues not ever? Yes, indeed... and if not ever... why haven't results achieved related to work therapy and costs related to work therapy been checked and evaluated, and done so recurrently? Fifth question! No, here in my case this is obviously so that not only people who have problems in the labor market but also decent tax prayers with a social conscience have been cheated! Who is held accountable if bad or no wrong performance related to work therapy does continue, then who is held accountable for also that lack of responsibility? I mean that tax money has to be spent within the limits of the law.

So, if tax money isn't a free utility... someone has to observe the law, and people and organizations under suspicion shouldn't be able to point at each other. Yes, and for all this is... The Ministry of Justice is responsible! Yes, also when Swedish authorities do ignore the laws! Yes, but obviously it's okay for some people to ignore the laws sometimes in certain situations in Sweden... and then especially it is okay to ignore the laws for less able people may tremble Swedish and wonder what next law the Swedish authorities will ignore.

Yes, this also goes for ethnic minorities with strange names. The members of the Swedish Parliament and especially the Parliamentary Committee of Legislation sure have the right to ask for feedback and information regarding all those laws being in force!!! They do not ask for that kind of information or very seldom! Oh, obviously then when no one is asking about feedback information... then, in reality, everybody is unaccountable... for example, related to this process of work therapy... and Lee SaLasso at "The National Audit Office" who has been supposed to check his old workmates and who knows and knew what was going on and he also knew that The Stockholm County Administration/Council paid Noman's wage money and who is then held responsible if costs for a certain purpose of work therapy are not met by significant achievements related to the very same purpose of work therapy; a work therapy which by the way is non-existing... and this lack of results are not shown after several years in the accounts and it is still not shown in the accounts wasted during those several years and nothing has been done about it! Hmm, criminal ulterior motives and County Councilor Leni Beginman and my unsafe salary and criminal ulterior motives which must be around.

Yes, I am talking about and relating to the purpose of work therapy! Does anyone take the minutes? No! Not when controversial issues and decisions and non-decisions are discussed! No one has so far been taking any interest in finding out about Skeleton's capacity regarding different work tasks! It's terrible! Desperation is growing! Waste of tax money! The Swedish Welfare State! Why have you abandoned Noman and the mic-people? Why do you spit on your own welfare laws? I am not alone in this!"

Roman Freud, the great psychiatrist did wipe the perspiration of his forehead as he stuttering said: 'Calm down. Oh, this is a difficult case! Especially, since the Swedish welfare bureaucracy is so damn well-meaning... in their humble appearance, hiding and hiding well some criminal ulterior motives and now this is nothing but a resting scandal of course! A resting scandal of deadly poison effect which is lying dog go in a cupboard or sarcophagus in the form of a Skeleton or why not a Mummy!!!! Yes, six years at BAD-Department which should have been six months, only. Hmm, some indication!! Yes, a deadly scandal being stinking and ready to explode. Oh boy! Is there something else we should know about? Perhaps, related to this, I don't hesitate to say it... scandal!'

I just hissed: 'Whooo can tell... Maybe I can, or let's hear somebody else. Sixth question! At BAD Cupboard Department they don't need to pay my wage. That is done by the Stockholm County Council/ Administration. What is the effect of this?'

Brat Worst: 'Well, during present rules of competition... those people at BAD Cupboard Department don't seem to have and have had any incentives to take advantage of Noman Skeleton as a factor of production, 027. So far the only result has been neglect of tax money being spent and waste of Noman's time. 027... Noman's lifetime. Yes, Noman's lifetime is but shouldn't... be some free utility, 027! I soon begin to spin around in my small shorts of, of empathy of course.'X-Ray Charlie: 'The Key-issue here is that concept named incentives!'

I said: 'That's right X-Ray Charlie because there has to be a reason for this waste-oriented staff management... waste of tax money and waste of time being dead time or in other words Skeleton time or skeleton time... and nice of you to show empathy, Brat. Hm, Roll Hamson of Roland Hanson didn't explain his strange staff management vis-a-vis me. Oh, it is something called ulterior motives and it is something called criminal staff management!

X-Ray Charlie: 'Yes, I'll prick up my ears if you secret agent 027 Dodger Warner now will tell us about this strange waste-oriented staff management... of this now in initiated circles called notorious BAD-Department. Oh, I really think there is a reason why they have acted as they have.' Roman Freud: 'Oh, then I really think we have to go back to the old masters like Sigmund Freud and Carl Jung. I am especially thinking of that libido and...'

X-Ray Charlie: 'Oh, those popular psychological explanations, always hiding the true ugly economic explanations! Listen to a top brain and secret agent like 027 Dodger Warner!'

I said: 'Yes, this strange waste-oriented staff management... regarding money and time. Where both my lifetime and tax money seem to be free utilities. What is the reason? Not only have these people at BAD-Department wasted many years of my lifetime, but they did also waste some tax money, or more precisely, there has been a waste of $50,000 as wage money for me during all those years before and around 1980. You may call that some deliberate and criminal embezzlement of tax money if you want since I have never so far been aware of any enough significant achievements within the limits of the law for me or the university.

In fact... the relief work was an insult to me... and the university didn't directly and in a legal way gain much, either... in fact very little, within the limits of the law! Hence, we can state the existence of the waste of tax money of my lifetime and the existence of criminal black pedagogy telling me that whatever I did... everything was in vain. Yes, the techniques of control and domination. Yes, this criminal Swedish regime seized me by my throat figuratively speaking... and I found myself in a terrible social life situation that involved blacklisting and deliberate criminal embezzlement of tax money and deliberate criminal embezzlement of customer time and criminal ulterior motives.. and inappropriate and criminal political influence must have been exercised by the present corporative non-socialist government and then I was made a hostage like a pawn given rise to situations of extortion... and then the Swedish authorities did hide people of foreign stock and terror who were informed about me, but of them, I didn't know. Hmm, now I have realized that this first Swedish non-socialist government since 44 years had got a face, and gosh... how ugly was it not! Hmm, some face being just a front for the regular government!!

Yes, this non-socialist Swedish government has acted criminally and does still act criminal! Oh, and that perfect of a strange Cupboard and BAD-Department, Christ Middler... he has spread around false information about me... and then rumors and slander and finally calumny did follow being at least indirectly supported by sex-talking Sunway Sweetiepie! Criminal! Gee, and then those Swedes seem to be very confiding and easy to fool... suspiciously easy to fool and as I said, Christ Middler has spread around false information about me, and then rumors and slander and finally calumny have followed.

Well, or anyway... this is the best thing this egalitarian red socialist Christ middler can do to preserve the status-quo situation, a status-quo situation which is built on embezzlement of money and time, and therefore this certain situation in itself is causing the embezzlement. Woe and horrors! Perfect Christ Middler is also an embezzler and so is also Professor Person. Yes, Perfect Christ Middler can do... to be criminally acting or to be criminally non-acting... and for these black reasons be criminally rewarded criminal career, criminal career.

That career of his Christ rewards where some of those are most important... to him, Christ. That criminal rewards will be favoring his own criminal is obvious when he, Christ Middler, works with budget matters together with Mr. Toby budget matters being in some hint like dubious way related to criminal ulterior motives. Yes, I guess it's obvious that there is a strong connection between budget matters and more precisely allocation of budget money... and that in some respects non-existing but still very cunning and result-oriented destructive Noman-related staff management at notorious BAD-Department - a BAD staff management being exercised and performed in a criminal way by Roll Hamson. Hm, a criminal black staff management and a criminal black work therapy and criminal budget rewards and criminal appointments and Roll Hamson and Mr. Toby and Christ Middler who no doubt are responsible for criminal wrongdoings and therefore under normal conditions should be punished. Hm, they were not alone in this!

Brat Worst: 'I see, as soon as his own career is at stake, then this socialist Christ Middler will forget all about both socialism and solidarity. However, from the bottom of his heart, he feels solidarity if he is allowed to show solidarity by spending other people's tax money, and thereby favor his own career. That seems to be this socialist Christ Middler in a nutshell! Is this also your opinion, 027?'

I said: 'Yes... and thank you for your analysis, Brat Worst, but I guess Christ Middler thinks it isn't nice to take part in a certain judicial murder, to participate in this part of dirty business. However, that's exactly what he is doing. As a logical consequence, Christ Middler must have been either threatened or bribed... and then probably only a bribe reward for his neglect of duty... while I then was treated like a leper for some reason or another.

Christ Middler's bribe reward was named promotion, pro-mo-tion. First, this Christ Middler got that perfect assignment, and then he now wants a permanent university lectureship. It's just a matter of time. Yes, profiteers and bribes and victims. Christ Middler is a perfect example of utility-maximizing home economics. Hmm, the necessary but non-existing acknowledgment of certain empiric data and the science of economics and the Nobel Prize.'

X-Ray Charlie remarked: "Probably, this way of bribes and corruption is the way this is how Christ Middler will get this kind of reward or rewards, and therefore and because of this... or at least this is one reason why you have mapped a certain pattern of relations. A pattern of relations which could, for example, explain the behavior of this Christ Middler, etc. Oh, those Swedish Social Democrats who just follow orders and/or instructions but in your case, Dodger mostly hints at being criminal, not because of some pattern of hints in chain relations."

I answered: 'Yes, a pattern of relations where one can find certain strange hint-like chain relations to both Swedish business life and Swedish political life where you then also, for instance, can find determined Muslims with brown elements of ideology like anti-Jewish feelings, fanatic totalitarianism, war-hysteria, Arab racial unity and the sword under Islam, nationalism, elements of socialism and maybe corporativism, political indoctrination, Fuhrer-principle, no democratic control, Anti-Americanism, etc... brown Muslims which seem to be around in Sweden in a suspect way, and they were also around also in that oil-producing neighbor country of Sweden named Norway... Yes, those Swedes sure have some connections of both business-like and political nature... with brown Muslims, and also do Swedes have such alike connections with red Russkies and even black criminals.'

Brat Worst: 'Well, if Sweden has such good connections with those kinds of countries...then there has to be something wrong with those kinds of countries.' I added: "Sure! You seem to be my mind reader, Brat."X-Ray Charlie: 'Yes, some network of dubious relations, which perhaps could be called "the League of three colors."

Everybody in chorus: 'Oh! All the commies are red. We will chase them until they are dead. People are criminals and black. We will then all track, and then also crack! All the Arabs do like terror, but we will be caught them when they do some error! Gosh! "The League of Three Colors!"

I felt slightly sick of all this American indoctrination, but I guess this was the only way.

X-Ray Charlie: 'Now, you have something more to tell us... haven't you, 027 Dodger Warner?'

I said: 'Yes! Now, as far as this Swedish bureaucracy is concerned and a judicial murder... what we so far have found are often only indications pointing at some pattern of relations linked to a certain effect where the effect is the judicial murder of Noman Skeleton, a case which we now all are talking about. Some case! In some cases where the closer causes to the effect can be spelled the budgetary process and the staff management! Oh, I also as a third cause have to point at those tight relations between different categories of people; like the different experts of human control, like psychiatrists, staff managers, etc. Then those experts have relations with other experts, bureaucrats, budget people, union people, business people, and politicians. In short... we have here different important categories of people in Swedish society with close relations to each other and who do form certain relations. Yes, a number of people belonging to those categories I just mentioned, and they had and have one lowest common denominator..."

Everybody: "Our excitement is endless! What is and has been the lowest common denominator between those different categories of the Swedish establishment?"

I answered: 'The lowest common denominator is... that those different categories of so-called fine Swedish people don't mind running criminal errands for people of real high power while they believe a lot of lies giving them some kinds of excuse... to for example use Noman Skeleton as some kind of blacklisted object for indirect... extortion, where Noman also should become a manipulation object which shouldn't be in the position to interpret the situation, the game-situation which include different red brown black places... to which and where the manipulations can take Noman. Yes, and then around some Cupboard at some BAD-Department, there are brown Muslims like Candidate Hassan Nadjafi from Iran and Candidate Amjed Babar and Candidate Moha Badran from Egypt, then there are red comrades like that Russkie Candidate Tavaritij Alexandrov and that Czech Candidate Zabrodsky, and finally I think Candidate Paavo Waltzer is related to some black drug gangsters. Well, that last statement, wasn't only a wild guess... I guess.'

Web Spooky: "Well, a close look at those people shouldn't hurt. Well, all kinds of hypotheses have to be tested. Hmm, "The League of Three Colors"... and that Swedish establishment... where the different categories of the Swedish establishment, all seem to agree about that... as you call it … status-quo situation at BAD-Department... which is nothing else but some very terrible situation of blacklisting for Noman and an awful situation for some other people who should pay some kind of ransom or interest of ransom time and time again, recurrently.... where then this Mr. Skeleton is available all the time or time and time again for negotiations of relentless extortion research-project or the like... a red-brown black related to some research-project which could be a trap of fatal nature; when the trap-door slam! Then, there exists no mercy for a mortal soul... if not the big ransom will be paid..." I said: "We, have to put forward and advance a certain hypothesis."

Brat Worst: "Which reads?"

I explained: "Stringon Pullman, is head or director general of the Swedish institution SPI, State Personnel Institute... an organization which may influence all public staff management, directly formally or indirectly informally, and he has a colleague at the Stockholm County staff management Administration being related to the County Councillor Leni N Beginman, and this Leni being a woman who among other things could focusing on medical and social issues and who for some ulterior motives is a salary giving woman related to a budgetary process. Hmm, a few times my salary paycheck didn't arrive for some reason or reason, but otherwise, always does it arrive for some other reason or reason.

Yes, that woman with red hair named Leni N Beginman is informed! Yes, the Swedish government and its budgetary process and its staff management will influence Stockholm County and its budgetary process and its staff management... and for some reason and also influenced will then be Dr. Borgenhammar and whoever is hospital president or maybe "acting hospital president" at The South Hospital and then also influenced will Dr. HerCo-Witch be... being head of MAD-Clinic at this very The South Hospital. Yes, thinking of Noman... there are here in Sweden certain people who are working together to reach a centralized totalitarian overall control point of view focusing on one individual only... on one human life only!! Yes, for those Swedes of corporative power, it is now possible to fix a directed focused total control over a single individual and thereby a single human life in the Swedish society... and this control can be of scientific nature... and this is my hypothesis!

Yes, that's a hypothesis that also can be advanced, and in the Noman case, we can also find some traces of how the national Swedish budgetary matter of finance or budgetary process of Stockholm County. Oh, this minister of finance or budgetary matters in the Swedish government named Ingemar Mundeboo and his colleague of the Stockholm County Administration, Bossy Ringholm. Hmm, I can assume that this is Leni N Beginman, county councilor, and then also director general for the Rationalization Institute of Hospital Care and her diabolic friend Bossy Ringholm are preparing something terrible in Greater Stockholm if and when something else of hostage-like nature will be lost... Hmm, hospitals and rationalization possibilities...'

Ramon Freud: 'Hmm, interesting I am as a psychiatrist very well aware of those organizations called... hospitals. I have noticed that sometimes the formal organization is one thing, and then the real organization is another thing. Yes, why not know it, but "The

South Hospital" may sometimes serve as an informal university hospital...'X-Ray Charlie: 'Right, an informal university hospital sometimes run by the Swedish State & Government, but "owned" by The Stockholm County Council. yes, formal university hospitals are in Sweden run by the State & Government.' Roman Freud: 'I and X-Ray should perhaps discuss "The South Hospital".' I replied: 'Yes, that informal university hospital. Hmm, a prostitute girl named Susan Anelli once told me about secret experiments involving electrical shocks for example going on at that very, The South Hospital, and scientific experiments and an informal university hospital. Secrets!? Roman Freud: 'Yes, informal experiments, taking place inside... some informal university hospital...'

I stated and added: 'You got it! Sometimes Swedish doings are very informal. Gee, people like Dr. HerCo-Witch at MAD-Clinic are being subordinated to Dr. Borgen Hammar and The South Hospital... plus people like Roll Hamson and Hunter Mabon, etc at BAD-Department being subordinated to Hardy Viceman at Monte Fresco University... Yes, all these people and organizations could be influenced by SPI and its Boss Director General Stringon Pullman, influenced in some informal way to exercise different forms of sophisticated control methods within the framework of some diabolic experiment or experiments.... of staff management.' Hunt Recardo: 'Black pedagogy and Electronic Data Processing can also contribute to...' I exclaimed: '... scientific enslavement of people...'Brat Worst frowned his forehead and said: 'That's right! This organization SPI will use not only methods in psychology, sociology, group dynamics, stimulus-response, sticks, and carrots, threats and rewards... but maybe later also methods of biochemistry and electronics... to drill certain employees.

Hmm, part of some extreme economic mechanical control thinking and I guess within the framework of staff management, or is it something else? Some kind of secret research is perhaps anyway going on. You know, being very small I and Douglas Boy have tailed those fellows from The Black Pedagogy Department and MAD-Clinic and BAD Cupboard Department... and checked their drive writers being secretly mounted on their cars. Hmm, I certainly have noticed how a small number of learned fellows are spreading around their knowledge to a somewhat, larger number of learned or powerful fellows... Yes, still a small elite group...' I added and explained: 'Hmm, elite discussions in different fields of knowledge between different experts giving new knowledge, being important also for staff management. Yes, and thus this new knowledge is spread out not only in secret discussions but also by secret unconventional courses delivered by BAD Department.

Sure, new knowledge could be distributed but should be spared public publishing... and the course package ought to be covered by courses designed in more conventional forms, designed like innocent conventional courses without any sign of the hidden new controversial information and then also for example without mentioning one word of those hidden discussions about that awful and criminal case study of Noman Skeleton going on, and not to be mentioned with one word should also other very controversial scientific experiments of staff management be... not one word outside the circle of initiated course members. Oh, that hidden black pedagogy and its hidden written-down results which can be found in secret courses! Hmm, and Noman Skeleton isn't the only one being unknowingly one being exposed to black science.' I paused and added: 'Hmm, innocent private teaching regarding innocent university courses... this constitutes the covers which taken by themselves may call for some comments, but then more important are those on the sly supplementary and those dubious on the sly courses telling about know-how related to economic criminal deeds being then also related to some criminal staff management which also exercise criminal experiments!'

I also added: "Yes, criminal Roll Hamson and his criminal staff management beyond the law which includes black pedagogy, involves blacklisting and techniques of oppression control domination and which can be related to criminal tests and one or several experiments, and then why not also criminal consensus experiments with actors also outside Sweden which make room for bribes influencing staff management and for options to political corporative influences... which may lead to extortion, and all that." I walked around the room looking at books on bookshelves in a sweeping way, and I shrugged my shoulders and I said: "Well, as a Swedish citizen I can't here in Sweden write about all subjects like taboo subjects... but having done some informal field studies in some Swedish institutions...

I here may have found experiments that start up at a local BAD place being also linked to some other place being somewhat MAD... and then options are given to local interests to influence me as not only a test person and study object but also a hostage pawn... local interests looking for advantages like some ST-union section at a certain university and then... these so-called local natural interests looking for advantages can expand both geographically and hierarchically … and in my case... we can here talk about an expanding field experiment and how things develop all the time until we have reached the top of the national corporative interests like for example that one umbrella union name TCO being led by Len Bodyswap or his successor Big Bear Rosengreen."

I then added: "Hmm, I am a test person and a part of a field experiment of a shaking moral kind; generating awful deeds which are of scientific concern and may be also of commercial concern?... I am like a mixed drink shaken, but what about stirred?" I paused and finally said: "Yes, we have experiments of scientific and even commercial interest... where involved are people at BAD-Department and MAD Clinic..." I finally-finally said: "Sure, experiments in staff management and individual ambitions, etc... and those awful matters of scientific and commercial concern are also discussed in a whispering way inside some to hundred percent sound absorbing BAD and MAD conference room, and in that BAD and MAD conference room, there are promises of secrecy..." I finished my monologue by saying: "Gee! Reality has it, that BAD Department is a strange deliverer of mysterious criminal courses and also mysterious criminal experiments."X-Ray Charlie turned to me and said: 'Amazing, you Dodger seem really to know these "Swedish bastards of power and their cronies." I remarked: 'Well, I only do observations and conclusions... and assumptions.'

Ramon Freud: "Yes, but all of us should by now just like Dodger here know these "Swedish bastards of power and their cronies"...

but we should even know them much better if you X-Ray Charlie should allow you to bring these "Swedish bastards of power and their cronies" into a scientific psychiatric laboratory clinic on secret suspicions alone for special torture like therapy... of BAD and MAD nature." I just stated: "Well, that powerful Swedish scum sure needs some so-called Swedish well-meaning therapy themselves while they look at themselves in the mirror and find out what kind of dregs they really are. Now, this therapy should take years and years until these Swedish dregs realize that there are worse punishments than death."

Web Spooky: "Oh, but before you have done some kidnapping and have reached that final point of preparation works with some vermin in human disguise being big wigs and some special living Swedish power-related guinea pig materials... for a scientific study, then allow me to give you some advice regarding sophisticated methods of interrogation. Yes, brutal if necessary."

Hunt Recardo: 'Well, if these sophisticated methods of interrogation should call for sophisticated electronic equipment, and I am sure those methods will then let me give you Dodger some pieces of advice regarding electronic tools may come first and then may new methods of interrogation be designed. Yes, and this means that you should contact me before you contact Web Spooky.' Web Spooky: 'My hat, how can you say that! Things work the other way, I would say! Again, my hat, how can you say that!'I said: 'He can't, but he says it anyway... because he obviously is some kind of salesman. Now, the interrogation has to be seen in its scientific context.

First, you do analyze the real situation of research or inquiry, and then you enlist the techniques which can be used which include criminal interrogation techniques, and what kind of tools then can be required. Yes, you enlist the techniques of interrogation, reconnaissance, etc... which can be used followed by some tools required, and then you do some selection/adjustments of tools and techniques to the situation of inquiry and thereby you should find the right method/methods given the present investigation situation.

Yes, and then you again analyze the situation of research and inquiry and line out the methodology and specify the methods and tools which should be used.. and then you again check the real situation and the methodology being lined out, and now I am just talking and have just been talking in general terms...”Brat worst: “What about tools of torture?... To be more specific.” I answered: “Sure, different kinds of tools will certainly be included... and when efficient... tools of torture have in certain investigation situations high priority! Such high priority that they can be improved!’

X-Ray Charlie: “Okay, talking about scientific methods... when this scientific psychiatric laboratory clinic is ready and the “Swedish bastards of power and their cronies” are kidnapped and captured... then I promise you. Roman Freud... that all adequate scientific methods of interrogation and all necessary tools of sophisticated electronics and chemistry and biochemistry will be available to you...”Roman Freud: “Good, and tools and techniques and methods of torture are no obstacles?”Web Spooky: “No, of course not.”I said: “That is the only way to make those Swedes see what they have done, and then these Swedes can learn to know themselves better... and understand what they have done to other people. Yes, we are just trying to be well-meaning like the Swedes. Maybe, we all here in "my" spy-Centre at The Solid Star Street are part of a World Conscience... also..."For some reason now heavy threatening clouds massed together darkening the sky... and the sun itself went into some kind of eclipse permanent or not... and a thunder ball of rumbling evils was rolling over all of us. And now we all fainted with minds... not unfamiliar with mean/cruel thoughts.

Chapter 4

THE MEETING ABOUT FIELD STUDIES,

where I am some kind of rapporteur... must continue as if nothing has happened

After some time all of us returned to a state of consciousness, again, Not, however...remembering some just in the present, strange divine change in the weather... some divine force which now was finishing some process of return to normal. I looked at X-Ray Charlie, Brat Worst, Roman Freud, Hunt Recardo, and Web Spooky and we decided to return to that point in time when we were interrupted in our discussion due to stormy weather and thunder... and we all waited until all minds had found their ways to return to that certain point of time in a certain discussion.

Web Spooky: "What's more, 027?"

I answered while being in some kind of brown study talk: "So far, some of all those Swedish dirty and tricky bureaucratic operations that are not accounted for in public have like in my case been initiated rather than carried out due to less visible hinting. Yes, some less visible hinting is orchestrated by that Swedish corporative-related state & government organization named SPI=State Personnel Institute, and then when it comes to me the hints of dirty and tricky bureaucratic operations of staff management were passed on The Board of Monte Fresco University and now these hints are carried out by the staff management at BAD Department... and then those dirty tricky operations are being and have been and will be perceived by Noman Skeleton being me or just now my alias Noman Skeleton being in fact, Noman Skeleton being me or my alias Mirrony Stuntman. Yes, perceive those operations of BAD staff management... and then in the end I interpreted those operations as both staff management harassment and experimental staff management operations. I also looked upon those staff management operations hitting me... as just a lot of indications that something was wrong, and was criminal... Yes, something was wrong and still is wrong and something was criminal and still is criminal! Yes, an institution of the state or I mean a government institution... like SPI may give informal discreet hints of staff management to other State Governments organizations like for example Monte Fresco University and BAD Department where a stinking cupboard is to be found for some bribe-like reason and is to be found... for some hostage-like reason. Now, when it comes to staff management operations... then one or many budgetary processes can be a tool of persuasion. Hmm, I interviewed someone called budget boss Furstenbach... in a sad and bleak dim way. Yes, and at BAD Department there are some additional indications that something is wrong... for example that journey of flights Toby's... to Theran via Moscow. Hmm, Stringon Pullman and black staff management and SPI=State Personnel Institute and that journey of Toby's... Theran via Moscow. Connections? I believe so.

A secret journey connected to shady business which of course could have something to do with this blacklisting and extortion being related to that, shall we say, a hostage-like pawn being Noman Skeleton. And here we have criminal staff management! Furthermore... the EDP specialist Dr. Nichols from the BAD Department has now been appointed professor. Odd? Well, there's always some relation to shady business! I wonder if the reason is this Dr. Nichols and his... taking interest in psycho-medicine and interrogation and taking a working part in how he can find new possibilities for Electronic Data Processing? And what about that Russkie candidate of Dr. Nichols?... Alexandrov. Hmm, what about Industrial Espionage and Management of Human Control? Well, Comrade Alexandrov did specialize in industrial economics and industrial organization... on the record.

Hmm, and then off the record Comrade Alexandrov did specialize in industrial espionage focusing interest on both legal and illegal Management of Human Control. Shady business! Yes, KGB and GRU and Human Control and EDP... in Sweden in some combination I suppose. Well, and then Dr. Nichols and EDP and staff management and Human Control. Hmm, some of my Noman "friends?" have been hired for jobs in red Moscow... like that diplomat Arne Walter and that engineer Ben Otis. That's no accidental occurrence! Shady Business! Yes, Shady business is going on. Well, here we have a lot of indications that something might be wrong!'

X-Ray Charlie: 'Some lecturer! Now, what about your conclusions, 027 Dodger Warner?"

I explained: 'Well, a possible conclusion is that my former roommate at BAD Department is a Norwegian named Hans Thompson who has connections to my former schoolmate of a Swedish high school college gymnasium now a Norwegian diplomat and named Arne Walter. Hmm, and another possible conclusion is that Professor Paul Frenkner is involved in some long-lasting secret research project regarding economic administration business buildings, and real estate... secret research going on at BAD Department... he has had and probably still has some contacts with Ben Otis being an acquaintance of mine and an expert on elevator-technology also in Moscow, and he was a member of that in Stockholm situated board of Building Matters. Well, if not so often direct contacts so contacts through go-betweens.

Yes, BAD-Department and visits to Russia and what has love got to do with anything like blacklisting and extortion! Now, there is at this place BAD Department... many a decision process related to appointments, projects, courses, and journeys going on... which is not fully accounted for... accounted for only to some extent if at all... Yes, if those appointments, projects, courses, and journeys have something to do with for example Moscow and a criminal regime in Iran... then I am mostly thinking of smuggling of high tech and smuggling of weapons... Well, then if possible, nothing which can trace these dubious relations will show up in the accounts.

Furthermore, I believe that Red Moscow had mapped me and that Red Moscow is seeking and already has been seeking to enroll me as some kind of red agent related to hostage-taking and extortion. Hmm, I have to realize what parts my relatives and acquaintances can play, are willing to play, and are able to play behind my back. Hmm, the Norwegian oil and Swedish weapons and business operations in the dark and journeys and messages... Hmm, my relative and/or acquaintance Bill Mcalister has worked in Norway... way back in the sixties...'

X-ray Charlie: "You just now mentioned something about projects, courses, journeys, and appointments being not accounted for to their full extent. Do you want to add some additional facts to those matters of secret hidden nature where I believe parts of those more or less hidden matters related to projects, courses, journeys, and appointments are likely to be criminal?"

I now nodded and then... using an overhead projector... I put forward a LIST OF ANALYSIS. The first headline was read PROJECTS

I then found out that I could just show some photos on the wall, and I said: "As a waitress at Arsta WindMill this certain young female journalist Strudel is supposed to serve Dr. Nichols and why not mix some soporific in a mixed drink and then she=Strudel should put into the mix a microscopic transponder in or slightly inside Dr. Nichols body... with a code corresponding to Dr. Nichol's identity. Yes, Dr. Nichols being involved in some projects. "

Web Spooky: "Oh, that might be risky. That fellow Dr. Nichols is smart. He may discover one microscopic thing or two. Anyway, what kind of equipment will your agent-seeker use?"

I showed a constructional drawing and related experiments as I answered: "This enlargement will tell you how this very small transponder in or somewhat inside Dr. Nichol's body will send radio waves to our agent-seekers in for example these premises or somewhere else."

Hunt Recardo: "Oh, the body of paradise will carry that very small transponder rather than clothes... then I am content. Now, obviously, these 027 fellows have done some homework."

Web Spooky: 'Yes, and did you expect something else? Furthermore, I take it to you, 027 Dodger... already have decided whom to shadow?'

I explained: 'Well, that is the question. You see, many a university teacher at BAD Department are or may be related to some kind of revolving door between the university being part of the public sector... and big finance and industry being part of the private sector. For instance, there were some auditors hired as university teachers at this BAD Department. Chartered accountants like Jörgen Schumacher, and also consultants, etc. Yes, and they have been hired also by big companies... or small firms related to big companies... Hmm, yes... and now I am thinking of a fellow like Dr. Samuelsen who was and still is connected to private enterprise as a consultant... to Datema and Nordic Electronics and LM Ericson. One of the teachers at the BAD Department, being named Max Endre, was also a financial manager of a big paint company, Beckers AB. Small firms of suspect nature were founded. For example... that Greek fellow from that so-called "The DATA Laboratory", Mr. Matiakis, and that fellow from BAD Department being a university teacher in accounting, Mr. Sandberg... those two fellows founded a more secret than public consultant firm. Furthermore, Professor Paul Frenkner was the leader of a more secret than public project named "Economic Decisions Related to Housing Business", a project related to powerful business interests, where some business interests were of private nature and other business interests were of more red collective nature. Quite recently; I also have found out that my beloved Professor Sunway Sweetiepie had certain assignments, like being the chairman of this Nordic Company... Yes, I think I just mentioned some names to shadow.'

X-Ray Charlie: "Oh, all this is very interesting information! Hmm, "Scientific minds?" And projects and scientists and their connections to mostly Swedish interests and some BAD people standing with one leg in the public sector of the Swedish society and then standing with the second leg in the private sector of the Swedish society and then these BAD people have been organized with ties to Swedish unions-labor corporative both as members(SACO) and in their research work (any union) and some of these BAD people have been organized with ties to commercial corporative both as members (own companies) or as representatives of members (representing some owner of a company) and in their research work (any company or any organized natural interest of commercial enterprise) and then all these BAD people have ties to one Swedish parliamentary political party... with one red China related Fair face exception..."

I said: "Yes, these BAD people at BAD Department are in many ways tied to the Swedish society and then they may have to think of their own career, and they may have to think of their children's careers... and now it's to think about all those so-called scientists at BAD Department and what has become of their so-called scientific integrity when they now are running with all those profitable and strategic and I would say criminal relations of theirs... with the Swedish political establishment, and with Swedish private enterprise and with different Swedish corporative like maybe many a commercial corporative or some corporative of tenants and the labor corporative which are a special kind of unions. Yes, a special kind of union that participates in some corporative councils of references being connected to the Swedish government's decision-making. Well, even if some corporative are more equal than others... this is something, which is every corporative's due when concerned every corporative being acknowledged and confirmed..."

Web Spooky now interrupted me when he said: "Okay, I know you can mention a lot of names regarding BAD university people and you have mentioned some names regarding BAD university people who perhaps ought to be shadowed because of strange behavior in this Noman case combined with one or a number of dubious swinging doors leading to this or that Swedish or part of Swedish private sector... sometimes via or through some government-related corporative organization... being linked to research.'

X-Ray Charlie: 'Yes, for a university teacher at BAD Department some public authorities may also serve as go-betweens or intermediaries to the private business sector like some research council... or BAD Department itself. Hmm, private enterprises, and their Public Relations and public corporative institutions like some economic institutions for example The Bank Inspection or The Stockholm Chamber of Commerce, etc... and the importance of utility-maximizing for private enterprise.'

I answered: "Well, X-ray Charlie, those Swedish authorities and institutions which in Sweden are in a criminal helping mood... are also in a formal way corporative authorities like some research council and some university board. Yes, those corporative at the board Sure, those... both public and corporative institutions or organizations can of course be related to many a PR-function of some Swedish maybe exporting Enterprise. Yes, and criminal helping mood! Yes, and then the so-called Swedish scientists are themselves tied in many ways to the corporative being representing the natural interests within the framework of the Swedish Nation. Yes, these Swedish scientists are really tied to political parties and Big Government and Private Enterprises... and corporative like labor-corporative and commercial corporative... Talk about the lack of integrity! Maybe... these so-called Swedish scientists are in lack of a mother who can support them with her pension money because then these fine scientists can integrity!"

Web Spooky: "Well, I don't mind if you should happen to be the best scientists, but I sure believe that you are a good enough scientist. Hmm. Now, you 027 Dodger Warner said that a number of dubious swinging doors between the public Swedish sector and the private Swedish sector were in ugly operation... and it sure seems to me that you, 027 Dodger, really meant that almost all these people in this your story are some damn good bad crooks, or what?"

I answered: 'No... that I can't say even if it seems quite possible. No, this would be to anticipate and forestall honest and serious conclusions... in this early stage of the investigation... but who knows? Maybe, to be corrupt... is a quality that you can't be without if you want to be an acknowledged scientist in this gloomy science of economics, in Sweden... I am afraid. Yes, and the conditions and the demands on economy journalists are even worse... I am also afraid.

Yes, why am I so afraid? I anyway think that most BAD scientists are prepared to become some damn good bad crooks... if the price/ benefits are right! At least some of all those BAD fellows must have been bribed. I guess other BAD fellows must have been threatened to do things they really wouldn't and shouldn't do, during normal circumstances... Hmm, and then I guess the university teachers talk themselves into a certain concept of thinking... false but convenient as it may be... for them! Yes, then we have this last category of Swedish BAD scientists often being socialists who claim they have very high ideals but then when dirty things happen... do they may still just do not see anything and just not hear anything and just not talk because these cynical scientists feel more comfortable in this way. Well, we all do our choices for example me... then in this our only life... but when the ugly truth is knocking on our door, are we then willing to stand up and admit responsibility for our choices.... or do we just want to sneak away and hide what about Swedish BAD scientists? Maybe these scientists can tell us about bigwigs of political and economic power in Sweden.'

Web Spooky: "Yes, I have also heard that almost everybody at BAD Department was bribed or could be bribed... and if threatened no one registered, at BAD Department. Yes, and then some convenient people who didn't want to get involved were also able not to get involved keeping their eyes wide shut. Now, I just do wonder how does this false concept of convenient thinking go?"

I answered: 'Like this. Why resist temptation and threats... if you don't risk any punishment when you neglect the proper performance of your true duty? If you just hide behind lawyers like Mr. Lawtwist and Mr. Forgemaster and Mr. Sandeye, then no one can charge you for neglect and/or wrongdoings. Yes, more than once... a corrupt Swedish court of law... have experienced manipulated proceedings, and better still... you may find the BAD factors of causes which create the conditions and ways of tricky arguing following cover-ups. Well, there at BAD Department by criminal deeds which now have turned BAD Department into Skeleton's Cupboard Department which means a nest of corruption and ulterior motives with swinging doors to money and power. Yes, and no honest soul can deny that... at BAD Department also nicknamed Cupboard Department... there are fewer threats of sanctions and more promises of bribes, around. Also, things can be arranged out of sight, and here in Sweden I have no witnesses who dare to back me and those public documents and public records which do exist are faked and do not correspond with the Big Truth and are therefore of no value to me. Yes, I guess I have mentioned several effects which have appeared as a result of a number of factors of cause. Sure, but this is my picture of the facts of the big truth received, which does not correspond with the public Swedish picture of the facts of the big truth. Karl Marx is now behind my shoulder telling me about the class struggle and their thesis upstairs at the House of Society... and then my anti-thesis... downstairs at the House of Society which I already knew something about. Hmm, according to the thesis the people upstairs could belong to the world conscience... and the people downstairs like me could be... sanitary un urgency!'

X-Ray Charlie: "Well, as far as facts are concerned... I agree with you, Dodger... and I also feel I should know this for sure, but can you

Dodger here in Sweden prove that what you say is for sure? No? You are shaking your head, No! I thought so. Anyway, having heard you Dodger... including your last silent answer... I certainly can see what you mean by 027 Dodger Warner and also I have some experience from Sweden. Hmm, enough indications should become evidence, if you ask me!"

Web Spooky looked at me and said: "Hmm, as the second man and next man to our DBIA boss Mr. Z... I happen to know that our agency DBIA sure is interested in many a certain kind of R&D work which somehow is related both to BAD Department or BAD Cupboard Department and some dirty so-called Skeleton related scientific projects at BAD Department being linked to R&D projects... all projects being connected to BAD Department, but projects which may take place outside Sweden in some red or brown or black country/countries where also a transported Skeleton one day might be found and those Swedish BAD scientific projects being linked to R&D projects... are somehow being at that kind of foreign place, and at that kind of the future point of time where also a Skeleton is more or less expected to arrive having signed for a projected voyage, but not yet realized.... and in this situation the threat of fatal mutilation/ castration focused on Noman Skeleton is connected to some kind of extortion and when we have this connection between threat and extortion and have it before the Skeleton may arrive and also before the Skeleton has signed for a red brown black deadly project voyage then we have a situation of gamble. Yes, the Swedes do in masked words threaten our DBIA clients... in this so-called before situation. Now, if in this so-called before-situation, some ransom or rather the interest of ransom can be paid, then the threat will be eliminated for the time being. Skeleton is shaken, but not stirred... or I mean not self-going! Gosh! Swedes, and criminal negotiations. Now, I would like you Dodger to give me just one example of bias research. One example to begin with."

I explained: 'Well, that shouldn't be too difficult... Hmm, I have no evidence as yet, but I think this Mr. Edby might be a reasonable candidate in that respect... of biased research. He is working on a report concerning cheap electricity... which includes electricity generated by nuclear power stations. Powerful interests are involved. Yes, some rational production of electricity pays attention to sunk costs in nuclear plants, and some rational production and distribution of electricity pays attention to how a privatizing of all sources of energy and the whole infrastructure of electric distribution how all this should and could be anticipated to result in cheaper and cheap electricity, but then what about all those risks costs not yet realized? What then about some Electricity Exchange? Buying and selling quantities of electricity? Will there be some efficient market? What about Oligopoly risks? What about Nuclear Power as a source of Energy and Ulterior Motives!!!? Hmmm, Swedish foreign policy and Swedish smuggling of possible weapon-related stuff? Gosh! Gee Man! Oh, I will let Yoke Course Sackoh shadow Mr. Edby. Hmm, Edby's research and finding some piece of truth here and some piece of truth there while another piece of truth is hiding in the dark and yet another piece of truth has been distorted by strange lightning. Well, I am just like Vladimir Lenin taking an interest in the electrification of society."

Web Spooky stared at nothing with a thoughtful expression on his face. He then said: "Yes, I am sure a scientist like this Mr. Edby being related to powerful circles, has to follow other rules than those of science alone. Hmm, research related to powerful interests and electricity costs and risk factors and ulterior motives... must be followed by some most likely... tricky considerations, giving biased research... Hmm, and all this shadowing you are prepared to initiate, brainy 027 Dodger Warner... you are trying to find out what?"

I replied: "Well, for a socialist and scientist there is at least some importance, to be honest... but if Guran Edby being a socialist and scientist now isn't honest... that is because he has realized the overall importance of being Earnest. Anyway, I am trying to find out about these important and especially Edby's important relations of communication and their place in that pattern of communication which make these Swedish BAD university chaps spin around... Yes, and as far as outlines of these so-called scientific projects are concerned... one may wonder how much of a certain project works... how much of the work process and the work results are accounted for in public... and how much is printed and coded... being kept in secret? Yes, BAD university people and their relations and patterns of communication with powerful people representing powerful interests!"

I now paused and made the overhead projector show the second headline which was read, COURSES. I explained: "Well, when there exists such information which according to some people can't be exposed to the light of the sun, then the risk is great that certain criminal relations and criminal patterns of communications will develop. That kind of hot information someone must cover and then cover up! Now, some cover consists of a number of so-called "decent" university courses. There exist also some companies where the interest in dirty lobbying sure is great enough. Yes, and the Swedish people of these kinds of companies can always smell a hostage-like situation and they can always exercise their lobby operations in darkness... not being obligated in Sweden to register their lobby activities. Now, those Swedish "lobby companies" have bought and still buy courses about taxation, staff management, marketing, and cost income analysis... from BAD Cupboard Department... and this buying of university courses takes place always for some wrong and suspect reason! When those so-called "external courses" being also here so-called covered courses take place... then there are probably secret discussions about the secret contents behind the cover, and then very often and suspiciously often there are discussions about that hostage-like situation which Noman Skeleton has to face at BAD Department, even if Noman himself hasn't a clear picture of that hostage-like situation... a hostage-like situation related to cruel blacklisting and extortion! Well, some Swedish business interests will always try to take advantage of any situation of opportunities which will emerge, criminal or not... and some Swedish people in public service let them, like some bureaucrats and politics and union leaders and university teachers.

Yes, having access to many a criminal advantage is nice, and tastes good. Swedes who are vermin in human disguise can tell... Moreover, promising economists working for big companies must also be in this or that criminal course to learn how they should cheat the tax man, how they can enslave people using methods of modern staff management... and also must they learn how they can take advantage of hostage-like situations when they use criminal methods of marketing. Yes, and Swedish criminal lobby firms involved certainly have considered strategies and possibilities during the present situation of legislation which should mean the influence of parliament decisions about these and those laws and authority government decisions about these and those rules and then the same Swedish criminal lobby firms of course and certainly have considered their client customer's needs regarding their business strategies and possibilities during some possible changed situation of legislation and changed rules. Not especially innocent courses including case studies... Hmm, some businessmen do hire lobby firms and study criminal university courses. No, not at all innocent courses, especially since due to achieved criminal consensus those courses also may be connected to Skeleton-related blacklisting and Skeleton-related extortion! Discussions about this will also take place. Hmm, I was never taught these dirty tricks in some external courses, outside the university, external courses which formally are supposed to embrace the same contents as internal courses inside the university... and when I passed my university courses I passed internal courses! When it comes to dirty tricks I had to find out everything by myself! This isn't fair! There must have been both a white visible fee and a secret invisible black fee... being paid for those BAD external. Gee, some BAD university teachers!'

Web Spooky made funny faces, especially some long ones while saying: 'Well, courses, looking through those glasses of your enemies... I would say... that then it's decent or is it not?... No, I guess that wasn't decent. I'll tremble for your enemies, 027. Eh, why don't you give me another lecturer, Mr. Filibuster?'

I remarked: "My enemies wearing sick glasses may tremble alone, Web Spooky... Besides, why should I give another lecture free of charge... when I am now working for this agency of business intelligence, DBIA!? I haven't been paid, yet! Hmm, who am I, a soul of vanity... to unveil a spooky web and network of criminal relations only by delivering revealing lecturers!? Still, this is part of my work; but when will I be paid?'

Web Spooky: 'Oh, what a terrible workmate who speaks like that, but still... you might be right Dodger."

X-Ray Charlie now rose to his feet and with a serious expression on his face he started to go forward and back as if he was Napoleon Bonaparte, and he said: Web! What's so interesting... this is the snowball effect that is caused by this Skeleton case, also influencing certain now heavily expanding and/or suddenly better-off American and Swedish companies which I as some kind of an American police auditor... have visited. Yes, using both true and false identities. Now, all this business expansion, etc. Sound suspicious to some businessmen outside Game Scorpio. Yes, and this hostage-like pawn or hostage-pawn Noman Skeleton is also called "the ice cream man" for some less decent reason. Sure, and this name together with that business-related so-called snowball effect does explain why a certain war has started up, a war named "the great global Ice Cream World War", I am afraid. Yes, this is no innocent or funny war and why don't you give us another lecture, Mr. Filibuster? Not free of charge!

Here, is some envelope with some money in it."

Web Spooky: "He, Dodger, is employed by DBIA!"

X-Ray Charlie: 'Sure, but someone... has to check DB IA's clients. Clients in Spree! Noman Skeleton has the right kind of motivation. 'He will work for the FBI on a temporary basis.'

I replied and lectured: 'Oh, I will now with this money fuel behind me start to tick and lecture, no offense Web Spooky, and I'll tell you, that it is a firm belief of mine that those course teachers from this BAD Cupboard Department, often did shift content and purpose of those their courses. Off the record of course. I am talking about the external courses. A course is a course but sometimes a course isn't what it seems to be. I mean, instead of "innocent" courses in economics there were at least also talks about blacklisting and possibilities of extortion in many a course some blacklisting and possibilities to extortion related to Noman, which meant to be a Skeleton... in the media buzz. Well, some calculating Swedish people like to exercise the art of how they through extortion should be able to line out and practice "unconventional" marketing being also criminal, and fix "unconventional" business deals being also criminal. Yes, those methods of "unconventional" marketing and "unconventional" creating of business deals... are of criminal nature. Sure, to be found are secret courses, talks, and then deeds, not so innocent. Some BAD Department with a stinking cupboard is always present... to give service to criminal Swedish business interests! Some corporative boards of the University of Monte Fresco are also around governmental service to Swedish business interests... just as also that dubious board of the ST-union section. Yes, Swedish criminal organizations and Swedish criminal consensus, and the backing of the Swedish export industry! Oh, mutual corporative interests constitute some National Interest. Hmm, BAD Department where BAD stands for Business Administration Department... and its criminal services to some criminal Swedish Enterprise, and then not only private business. Of course, all this can't or shouldn't be, according to ideals, ethics, and moral but empirical data and reality says otherwise! Yes, it is no doubt some very great shame to this Swedish BAD academic society that these kinds of "unconventional" discussions about extortion related business deals are allowed to be... and take place within the framework of criminal course deals, are hidden behind... Hmm, so-called "innocent external university courses" are undercover. Yes, shame on you... BAD Department! Oh, I suppose you now understand why we who are working for DBIA really do need to exercise some illegal counter-espionage activities... focusing on these suspect and obscure courses at BAD Cupboard Department and those illegal counter-espionage activities authorities which are participating in and around should be demanded by and initiated by DBIA's client companies and those illegal counter-espionage activities should among other things be focusing on these mostly Swedish companies and these mostly Swedish linked to BAD Department. Yes... and outside those BAD courses, these suspect and obscure courses at BAD Department and their extortion-related influence for Swedish criminal companies and therefore very helpful and also for Swedish criminal authorities which might lead us to Swedish high-tech related espionage, for example in the USA, and then also and maybe most of all to Swedish high-tech smuggling and all this these BAD Swedish crooks can do... with some help of some hostage-like pawn at that BAD Department. Hmm, and the Swedish unions sure do participate in this criminal game! Yes, and with the courses do follow certain secret hidden Swedish letters of criminal privileges... Yes, and there is in some national Swedish interest that those letters stay secret.'

X-Ray Charlie: 'Someone must have read some papers of mine and put two and two together including some guesswork. What about you, Dodger?'

This chartered accountant X-Ray Charlie was in his uncanny mood when he also said: "Yes, and now I also guess we have to exercise illegal counter-espionage involving methods like burglary and kidnapping related to key reports and key persons, etc... being methods which can be called the last resort for an auditor or chartered accountant! Oh, how have I not wished to take such risky actions many a time myself! How are you gonna do it pal?"

I suggested: 'Well, we can begin with start to use the technique of wiretapping at BAD Department or at The DATA Laboratory where we have those wire boxes connected to this QZ computer central. We can just use a pair of cables, a small computer and a recorder, equipment which is supposed to turn on recording when certain lines... are connected. We can... Eh... fix that theoretically.'

Hunt Recardo: 'Really? Well, I better check your competence, then.'

Old Web Spooky now scratched his head and mumbled: 'Of course! This can be done! Of course! Hmm, I hope those strange Swedes do not talk in ciphers.'

I answered: 'Well, in that case, we have to crack the code.'

Web Spooky had a silky voice when he said: 'Sure! You will fix everything! Do you want to have those strange small microphones, walkie-talkies, and mobile car telephones at your disposal as well?'

X-Ray Charlie: 'Oh boy! You will cost the agency a lot, old boy! Dodger-boy! Therefore, you must be really good as an agent, 027 Dodger Warner. Yes, you better be real good! Expensive toys! Not to mention all those expensive investigations you are pushing for consuming many hours of labor.'

I answered: 'Well, now I want you to stop complaining all the time! Yes, and all this high-tech is necessary when you for example perform switched shadowing and simultaneous shadowing in certain situations, not only on the roads, but also in the air and in unclear water. I am serious about this! Yes, I may have to learn one thing or two and I need to discuss cost cuts so what? Stop it! I mean this complaining! Please!

Brat Worst turned to Web Spooky and X-Ray Charlie and the other strange guys including me, and then he said: 'Yes, 027 is damn serious, and don't you dare to talk about toys because we who are working for DBIA are all true professionals!'

When everybody understood that it shouldn't be that easy to question and laugh... at that opinion of mine, not after that last remark of Brat Worst, then I again put forward that list of analyses... stressing the third headline, JOURNEYS.

I said: 'Well, I have at BAD Department noticed Mr. Toby and his journey to Moscow and Iran. Maria Headwall and her journeys to Yugoslavia. Akin Sellerin and his Journey to Italy, Paul Frenkner's journey to Austria, Lea Lucifer Person's travels to Brussels, and Sunway Sweetiepie's journeys to the USA. Foreign candidates like Hassan Nadjef from Iran and Amjed Babar plus Moha Badran from Egypt and the Egypt Embassy may have done trips outside their home countries and outside Sweden. Foreign visitors from the USA like Professor Metoff and President Pickodolly Binocular have made trips to Sweden, especially Professor Metoff. Furthermore, dr. Nichols nowadays stays in Helsinki and his Russkie candidate for the doctorate named Alexandrov has been traveling to the Soviet, probably now and then, etc. Yes, there are many journeys being made and a lot of attempts being made to reach international agreements... involving some kind of secret deals and there's for sure a demand/ will in Sweden to take advantage of every opportunity available, even the criminal ones. Hmm, secret international deals due to traveling wheels and criminal deals... and a BAD Department and some Skeleton in the cupboard, or why not a sarcophagus. Yes, some journeys... some criminal agreements! A lot of traveling people who could be traced!'

Old Web Spooky puffed on his pipe and mumbled: 'Yes, I understand that you 027... to some degree have watched those so-called humans traveling elements who you just now mentioned, and hopefully you have watched and you will watch certain phenomena tied to those certain journeys of theirs, those traveling elements, certain journeys which not always have been on the record, not to their full extent or not at all..."

I almost ensured: 'Well, we might find a pattern in all this.'

X-Ray Charlie: 'Yes, you better do, 027! Because if you don't you will soon vanish into thin air. What else?'

I then added: 'Yes, after you have vanished into thin air. Now, I want to stress another suspect side of the bribe phenomenon.'

I now again showed that list of analyses and stressed the fourth headline, NEW OFFICES.

I then lectured: "I think there were some hidden motives when Dr. Nichols got him... acting professorship in Finland, because maybe he then could contribute to some high-tech smuggling by testing equipment in some more undistributed way, helped also by his workmate and so-called disciple... red Tavaritij Alexandrov. Hidden motives were also around when Sunway Sweetiepie got her professorship in consumer economics at "The University of earLunarians", I guess. Yes, because then and therefore Professor Sunway Sweetiepie was moved from Monte Fresco University to that storm Centre named BAD Cupboard Department and some Skeleton... a Skeleton who was placed in a sarcophagus-like Cupboard near the very hypo-Centre-of the coming stormlike earthquake inside BAD Department... and the coming stormlike earthquake is unstoppable! Yes, Reader Sunway Sweetiepie was transported or moved and become Professor Sunway Sweetiepie. Yes, and one fellow who got himself involved in a coming possible stormlike earthquake is Christ Middler who once was running for an assignment as perfect of BAD Cupboard Department, together with Dr. Mabon, Dr. Shyburger, and others... and then the staff of BAD

Department was allowed, in some true corporation democratic spirit to choose the least qualified fellow for that perfect assignment, and the least qualified fellow was Christ Middler, from the Stockholm suburb named Snakeby! Yes, it was a democratic decision... to choose the least qualified man, being then easier to control for the employees. Hmm, democracy and matters of convenience. Still, some Skeleton was and is generating yet some rotten stench... which is related to that appointment of Christ Middler... to his noble perfect assignment. Yes, strange BAD institution democracy at BAD Department and criminal advantages at BAD Department... and this combination of democracy and criminal advantages have already taken place and will continue to generate a BAD rotten stench from a Skeleton... and this rotten stench from a Skeleton will then follow all those BAD democratic university chaps at this now more and more notorious BAD Department. Gee, I do here state that this Skeleton Stench doesn't abandon those BAD democratic people just because they have gotten so-called strategic jobs outside the university... like for instance that chap Leif Widen working for BooforceAB, Max Endre working for BohlinsAB. Hmm, BAD appointments in the private enterprise outside the university and BAD Department, and still those BAD appointed people who do smell like hell can't get rid of appointments linked to BAD Department in a dubious way of some stinking Skeleton, hiding in a Cupboard! Then, there also were new appointments related to government authorities, like in the case of Lee SaLasso now working for... The National Audit Office checking Monte Fresco University and BAD Department of all places! Also, do we have that professorship of the University of earLunariens going to Sunway Sweetiepie. Yes, and then also these BAD people now at new offices in different authorities outside BAD Department... did still after having left BAD Department to smell like hell because they couldn't get rid of some Skeleton stench. Hmm, new offices for BAD dubious services could be related to criminal marketing (Booforce, etc) and related to possible criminal financial operations (BeckersAB, etc), and related to criminal audit conniving (BohlinsAB, etc), and here we can trace some "foot-prints" to the same stinking Skeleton hiding in a cupboard. Gee, this is true if Mr. Skeleton is wearing The Ring of Dark Opportunities because then all evils are circling around him. Hmm, strange that I was around, and as of now my alias still is around at BAD Department... since the BAD guys at BAD Department didn't seem to want to invest in my competence, at all. Now, many of those appointments already occurred... have occurred, because those university folks have delivered and were expected to deliver corrupt services, also sometimes leading to some judicial murder. Sure, the judicial murder on me and my rights! Yes, BAD people in the Swedish public sector do carry out certain corrupt criminal services being often more or less indirectly suggested by private Swedish business interests, especially when mutual corporative interests are alive and in existence, mutual corporative interests expressing themselves also in discussions between private companies and the public authorities and these then criminal BAD people in the Swedish public sector must be rewarded! Hmm, BAD Department and criminal services from there to Swedish enterprise and BAD people being rewarded. Yes, we can find criminal corrupt services being related to a hidden stinking Skeleton being kept in a cupboard. Yes, and when it comes to the Swedish unions like the ST-union... people there like BargoSmith and KarinWestdole they can also deliver corrupt services... to other members of that ST-union than Noman Skeleton! Yes, and to other members of that whole umbrella organization named or rather shortened TCO. Yes, and at BAD Department... there was that union of academics with the initial letters SACO and those SACO people were also able to avail themselves of my=Noman's miserable situation. Hmm, that ring of dark opportunities... The Rong of Dark Opportunities... was a ring of strangling nature, like that serpent ring named... anaconda ring.'

Web Spooky: 'Oh my! Some lecture! All this sounds more and more suspicious. Black pedagogy! A ring of dark opportunities. Are there more horrible things you have to tell me, or us?'

I said: 'Sure, we have now come to or arrived at the fifth headline.'

I then stressed the headline AUDITING on the list of analyses The fifth headline.

I explained: 'You know, I have just as you... got some strange feeling and much more than a feeling that Noman Skeleton has been some kind of negotiation object and, possible indirect trade object if you will... and a wager object and an object of betting. Hmm, and a sex object... at least before... If so, some Swedish private companies which cultivate some international relations may... find an interest in Noman... and then these Swedish private companies may try to influence how the teachers/professors at BAD Cupboard Department... judge Noman Skeleton... and they judge Noman in this way or that way according to a pattern which turns Noman into a hostage-like pawn and this criminal influence which those criminal Swedish companies exercise... together with that criminal influence being exercised by criminal Swedish labor corporative and criminal commercial corporative... where both those categories of criminal corporative have seats in "The Board of Monte Fresco University" and all this corporative influence will therefore totally corrupt BAD Department and its scientific teachers and tutors. Hmm, auditing under some influence of powerful interests and a spineless character working for "The National Audit office" checking his old workmates and buddies with his eyes wide shut! Lee SaLasso was the name! Yes, the whole Swedish government and the important national corporative in Sweden have made Sweden a prison for Noman Skeleton!'

X-Ray Charlie looked at me and said: "So, and then you perhaps also mean and try to tell us, that the arrows representing fears of sticks and the arrows representing temptations of carrots both these categories of arrows have and will be piercing worried Swedish hearts of BAD people... arrows being sent from certain international business relations... and these international arrow relations of fears and temptations have obviously given rise to some kind of strategic national Swedish multi corporative pressure. Well, a pressure that will be reproduced in the BAD Swedish public sector and then also hit those professors at BAD Department or BAD Cupboard Department. Sure, those professors at the BAD Department who were then under the influence of some strong wave of pressure always put forward a negative judgment when this Noman Skeleton tried and tries to prove himself. Yes, that's how you think! You hence mean that the scientific signature has been for sale when it comes to BAD Department and Monte Fresco University, for sale for some reason or another. Awful, well, why shouldn't then some signature of auditing also is for sale at "The National Audit Office". Reasons for sticks and criminal sanctions and reasons for carrots and criminal bribes... can make people do just anything! That's your hypothesis, is it not?'

I answered and lectured: "Well, just about if only the temptation of bribes is big enough and the fear of sanctions is strong enough, and this sale of the scientific signature is an example to confirm this my hypothesis which has to be some preliminary hypothesis of mine, growing stronger and stronger. Yes, the Natural Law of Sticks and Carrots can express itself in some extremely strong uncanny way according to my hypothesis... and this hypothesis is more and more confirmed according to my opinion. Hmm, also Lee SaLasso's sale of his signature as an auditor... does confirm my hypothesis about how sticks and carrots can change Behavior. Yes, and most Swedes do very easily and fast adapt to criminal behavior giving just weak forces of sticks and carrots for some reason these strange Swedes have an interest in doing what they are doing, and what they are doing isn't nice. Dubious incentives and ulterior motives and then they are coming those Swedes of dirty deeds of no moral or some distorted moral... including false testimonies and severe calumny. Furthermore, when things are as they are and no auditor wants to pull the alarm bell; despite the fact that the auditor is responsible... whose name is Lee SaLasso... knew that irregular things occurred at BAD Department... that decisions and in the Swedish lawbook written down artificial laws were neglected... Yes, despite the knowledge of the existence of those dark facts that auditor from "The

National (Swedish) Audit Office" named Lee SaLasso didn't pull the alarm bell... When all these facts do exist for real and no correction mechanism is released, then you have to ask the same question as Dr. Watson... "What's on ". Well, someone has to ask that question! Yes, for instance, Lee SaLasso who now is supposed to control his good old friends at BAD Department where to be found in some very stinking BAD Cupboard. Yes, Lee SaLasso who is working for "The National Swedish Audit Office"... is also of great interest. So is also the recruitment of Lee Anderson from the BAD Department to this audit firm BohlinsAB. Hmm, Swedish private companies have initiated links to BAD Department where blacklisting and extortion are taking place and then we have auditing of deliberate neglect by Lee SaLasso who should focus on authorities. Also, blacklisting and extortion are taking place and can take place because the criminal links between BAD Department Swedish companies are not examined by Lee SaLasso!!! Yes, and then I am thinking of that auditing of deliberate neglect by Lee Anderson who should focus on private companies and their BAD behavior related to the BAD Department. Yes, criminal auditing! Sure, criminal auditing related to BAD Department... with links both to authorities and to private companies some criminal auditing carried out by both Lee SaLasso and Lee Anderson... who both had been recruited to audit organization from BAD Department. Yes, hardly some coincidence, I would say. Well, both accounting and auditing at BAD Department could be criticized, more than criticized...'

X-Ray Charlie suddenly become aggressive and now he therefore shouted: "Upon my honor! What a forbidding way to try to stop the noble art of auditing! Well, they won't stop me! Anyway, what can you expect from a bunch of Swedish government-related smugglers who have such high ideals which in this or that situation can justify crimes if you use this and that argument... of high ideals!! Yes, these kinds of smuggling Swedish criminal do-goodies participate in high-tech smuggling, and then at least I do wonder if these Swedes have Spirit connections to the Devil! Hmm, the Swedes say that American high-tech should be spread to poor countries because of solidarity reasons free of charge. An argument of the Devil himself! I am referring to this recurrent Swedish smuggling of American high-tech!... Yes, you know that both the CIA and FBI have called me in for a certain auditing job... and I think I have experienced those dubious Swedes in that auditing work of mine! Swedes, they make me throw up!'

I replied: 'Hmm, Swedes commit crimes and then they pretend as if nothing has happened. Now, however, you people will help me see to it that certain Swedes won't get away with certain crimes, won't you?'

Web Spooky: 'Yes, but the reason why we are here is not to help you in the first place, Dodger... instead we want you Dodger... to find new information and preferably some pieces of evidence which would serve as a point of departure to "The Harbor of Truth" for the great coming auditing work of our great chartered accountant here, Mr. X-Ray Charlie!'

X-Ray Charlie: "Are you service minded?"

I added: 'Yes, like when it comes to information services... but rather not services based on participating observation. I can per se do it since some bribing fellow American clients and principals already have done it. I mean these bribe-offering American fellows of ours have done participating observations I mean that all our principals do participate in a game on different and especially high levels and they sure, studying the Swedes, do bribe-related observations, participating observations. Well, I am talking about a game within Game Scorpio. Yes, a game above my level. Sure, and then there will be another game level where I am a part doing among other things participating in observations I could, and their possibility, that I could be fooled away to the wrong place giving possibilities will entice Swedes into criminal behavior... which perhaps then will become my specialty. Hmm, sounds to me like a dangerous specialty, but I guess that's just an odd fate of mine... which makes me think of... "the natural economic law of opportunity and risk". Yes, a natural economy should tell us that big possible profits waiting around the corner tend to make people less precautious. Yes, I was chasing my utilities and other people like Swedish and American businessmen were chasing their utilities, perhaps in a less precautious way... Yes, and the Swedes will be less precautious if those dubious Swedes now on top of every also are fully or hundred percent convinced... that they can minimize their own risks due to the fact that they, according to themselves... have full control over some hostage-like Skeleton some hostage-like Skeleton who is wanted perhaps in Washington or somewhere else in the USA for some strange reason. Yes, and the reason may have something to do with a resting scandal, not meant to become public... and/or...? Now, having said what I just have said... then this means that it is possible to arrive at some very profitable bargain, involving also only small risks for the Swedes. Yes, big dazzling profits and small risks, and why should then anybody be surprised when... the Swedes during these conditions very soon occasionally forgot and still forget to be precautious. Gee, but small risks are still risks and if they occur I hope they will become fatal! Hmm, big dazzling profits and small risks do not easily correspond with mechanisms of "the natural law of Opportunity and Risk"!

I paused and then I noticed that my audience wanted me to add something in an explanatory direction, and I then said, added, and explained: "There is here some gravitation factor related to big dazzling profits which will influence the risk. Yes, we have a gravitation factor here in that sense that much gold and much sheep entice many fortune diggers and beasts of prey out for dazzling profits and mutton do just follow their true nature, but on the other hand... the Swedish behavior is criminal! Hmm, criminal behavior is also linked to the natural law of opportunities and risks. Well, the concept of risk may contain many risk factors. Now, recalling my course books in economics... I don't remember anything written about "the natural economic law of opportunity and risks", and now I wonder why?"

X-Ray Charlie: "Well, talking about that natural economic law of Opportunity and Risk... I then guess I should tell you that I have noticed that people in Swedish... in Swedish business life no longer are as precautious as they once used to be. Well, certain Swedish businessmen do know that they can profit from a certain hostage-like situation, due to criminal services being delivered by this fine but still criminal, and very BAD, and why not MAD Swedish Corporative

Welfare State and even if they aren't many... too many people now already seem to know that is going on."

I said: "Yes, too many and not always so precautious... are those opportunistic Swedes and this is something that we have to consider while we prepare, plan for, and carry out some if necessary criminal field experiment contemplated... a most likely criminal field experiment which starts and has its origin in this wonderful Swedish idyll. Now... in fact, it's quite simple..."

Everybody: "Really? How?"

I lectured: 'Well, let just the Swedish authorities succeed with their sophisticated way of handling social elimination... harassing Noman Skeleton into leaving his so-called employment at the notorious BAD Department and thereby driving the unemployed Noman Skeleton into the arms of some psychiatrist and then drive this Skeleton or what's left of it into the arms of a criminal gang. Noman can then be a plaything without human rights... ready to please the upper classes in one a slave, and also run some criminal errands. Maybe, with Irish coffee as fuel. Well, I am here in some odd ways talking about some still very common social elimination hypotheses where way or another people must be humiliated and take risks... and if people still can't fit in society or the society won't let them, then some devil and his gang are waiting for those unhappy souls. Now, we want to test these simple hypotheses scenario or this simple theory by designing some kind of experiment, won't we? Won't we!!!'

Web Spooky: 'You really mean that?'

Hunt Recardo: 'This experiment could be interesting from an

electronic point of view, I want to stress...'

Brat Worst: 'I am also around, and most suitable for certain odd jobs which demand not the great jobs which demand not great agent, but the small agent.'

I said: 'Now, talking about my experiment, contemplate... if the Swedish authorities possess something somebody else wants, then the Swedish authorities won't let that something, and that something is me, just walk away. steps will be taken! Hmm, this "my" experiment is interesting... also from that point of view... that we now are testing institutions of power more than in some sense powerless individuals who have to play their two different parts in life... their part of a consumer and their part of a worker and maybe something more whatever this could be.'

I paused and then I added: 'Yes, an interesting experiment, and being part of this experiment is a shadow squad contemplated, and someone... and maybe I myself... have to design and specify the demands on the manning of the shadow squad, and then I should do some recruiting... filling the shadow squad list with names of real physical persons... of interest. Yes, and then these so-listed agent people will during an ongoing field experiment send spinners of messages according to some dark courses of events around me=Noman Skeleton take place. Yes, around me being Noman Skeleton courses of events will take place, and then active must this process of reconnaissance be a process of reconnaissance for the shadow squad where I should be the decoy and some kind of not chemical but socio-economic catalyst which thus release changes in the environment. Yes, indeed... have here many a process of reconnaissance of a field=area around me=Noman and now we as soon as possible have to discuss this list of those very members which we have to enroll... to my shadow squad, and how before it's time to leave this library and spy Centre at Solid Star Street and do some field studies. Yes, I am concerned... I have to leave with some kind of washed brain! Oh my, what a terrible field experiment!!'

Web Spooky: 'We know the torments of your heart a Centre of fear, poetically speaking, great Skeleton.'

I said: 'Yes, after some hypnotic brainwork, part of my present memory will cease to be. I am not to be, but still, I am to be. I am in a strong feeling of despair which shakes me down. Please, stand by my side... you always present Holy Spirit... when I now accept this terrible field experiment. I pray to you and fold my hands.'

Web Spooky leaned towards me and whispered: 'Hmm, I suppose that you 027 do realize that your true and old identity really... is Noman Skeleton... and in this experiment that you now are talking about you will be used as some kind of guinea pig & decoy. Hmm, suppose you soon will really quit at The Monte Fresco University, and try just to leave this awful country, Sweden... and then in that kind of process you and all of us must watch and observe what the Swedish authorities will be up to.'

I answered: 'Yes, it's interesting to watch that process of how Swedish institutions do behave and then also behave in a criminal way, but it's less pleasant to participate in that same process... as a guinea pig & decoy. Now, if I am trying to leave the strange Welfare State of Sweden which you suggest, and which I feel for doing when desperate, then those Swedish policemen or some other people may try to lay their hands on me... and when they do, then they will shake the truth out of me and if there still is some hidden truth left these Swedish policemen will kick it out, using more or less sophisticated methods. I, therefore, think it would be better not to know anything. Hmm, Swedish policemen who don't act in police uniform and don't show their true identity and who don't tell anybody that they really are policemen, they really are dangerous and very efficient when they worm out or kick the truth out of people. The problem is that I am in such a dangerous "kick out the true situation" or "worm out the true situation"... now know a lot of interesting facts, etc being of value to our Swedish enemy side, alright. I am an agent for the agency or DBIA, remember!

Web Spooky: 'Oh, but that is a problem which I or somebody else will take care of!'

Web Spooky now turned to those always present fellows, Roman Freud and Hunt Recardo and Brat Worst and also to X-Ray Charlie and me... and Web Spooky told us all that this agency of Business Intelligence, DBIA... had suggested that I should go into hypothesis in order to wash out my new identity from my memory my new identity as now the secret agent 027 Dodger Warner. Yes, I as Noman Skeleton should get some specific agent knowledge out weeded including my knowledge about Mirrony Stuntman, Brat Worst, etc. being part of my agent knowledge, this specific knowledge being accumulated and possessed by me in my capacity as agent 027 Dodger Warner, that specific kind of knowledge should be out weeded... washed out of my memory. All my memories as an agent of 027 Dodger

Warner should cease to be. Yes, Roman Freud now being present was probably really good at hypnosis. Now, this was a somewhat arbitrary and high-handed DBIA suggestion being delivered by Web Spooky which wasn't favored by me, on second thought, at least, not when I myself should be driven this far as guinea pig! As decoy! Me, Noman Skeleton, I should go around with part of my memory "the 027 Dodger file", locked into an invisible Cupboard... This suggestion made me hesitate, but what was the alternative? Another suggestion that however was favored by me and which also was put forward by Wed Spooky... was the idea of a shadow squad that should follow and check if something dangerous could happen to me if some very scary situation of immediate nature should appear, if so then this shadow squad should, without hesitation, interfere... and if no immediate danger, then the shadow squad should interfere... at an appropriate point of time, but how far could I trust this shadow squad?

I now read about tests related to this experiment of memory wash and then I checked those tests... before I did agree that parts of my memory should be washed out by hypnosis, at least for the time being. I also examined a rough outline of the shadow squad. Roman Freud now also ensured that these parts of my memory called "the 027 Dodger file" could be recalled. Well, I wasn't in the position to say no, and some moments of silence had risen.

After a while which appeared longer than it should... Web Spooky said: 'Well, 027... I take full responsibility for having persuaded you to go along with quite a risky field experiment in this strange case of yours.'

Roman Freud: 'I will also take some responsibility... upon my shoulders.'

Web Spooky: 'Hmm, is there anything more you want to add... Dodger?'

I sighed as I answered: 'I shall also think to Hun Recardo here... about that list of equipment which I just have lined down.'

Hunt Recardo: 'Yes, even if I have been around taking full responsibility, I am asking you... what have you> What have you?'

I answered: 'Ehh, what do I have? Okay... let's think... I have no specifications of all those things we now have mentioned, for example, different parts of radar equipment, bulletproof vests, laser sights, etc., hmm... plus shotguns of course. I have no specifications of figure pins, striking strings, channels in the gun tube, and data about revolving bullets, etc... and don't know if I should have. I and you Hunt... we have to discuss the specifications and fix all those requirements we need somewhere. Yes, both for me and the shadow squad.'

Hunt Recardo: "Well, I have some suggestions and arguments regarding specifications and where to turn with our requirements and you Noman are entitled to say... yes! I am positive! I am serious about this.

I answered and explained: "Hmm if you are serious... why are you then trying to be funny at my expense!? No answer? I'll remember that insulting attitude of yours while I have to suffer and expose myself to risks during my agent mission and I never forget it! Anyway, that shadow squad must be big since it probably will need to be divided during the operations, operations like the shadowing mostly. This shadow squad should not only watch and shadow and protect me, but they=The Shadows of the Shadow Squad should also at some place stay put when I=Noman is as meant to be, an experimental object being harassed and illtreated while the danger just isn't too high. Moreover, shadowing should be applied when it comes to people showing up and taking interest in my person and then leaving, but to where... while my runabouts do continue. Yes, these kinds of complicated shadow situations will occupy some manpower. Now, since I am taking and will be exposed to great risks here because of this I should be entitled to have a say... both when it comes to specifications of equipment and when it comes to specifications of manpower... and rules for shadowing and protection of my person.'

Everybody did agree with me how terrible this field experiment really was or rather should be and that I therefore should have a say when it came to specifications of equipment and manpower and rules for shadowing and my protection... and then everybody mopped some cold sweat off their foreheads and looked at me with long faces. Money and job opportunities were the big issues to shadow worry about and my life was the small issues to shadow worry about. I could feel it in my bones. The preparations for this risky field experiment now began to take form. I should now soon act using my own old identity only... Noman Skeleton! I was now shown photos of my alias Noman Skeleton... in his regular BAD weekday or... Yes, Mirrony Stuntman. The shadow squad and sets of equipment were built up and many days passed... Finally, I could say okay to both to the shadow squad and the sets of equipment. The final step in this process of preparations... was for me that scary therapy hypnosis.

*See Epilogue Volume III

I was now hypnotized by Roman Freud into some kind of dream-like state of mind, where now something told me to forget certain things I had seen and heard and concluded in my new capacity as a DBIA agent, as 027 Dodger Warner... because in this way I should become some kind of living ignorant bait for the fishing carried out by "my" shadow squad... I desperate ignorant bait meant to fool those Swedish and Swedish related fish=enemies of mine who wanted to take advantage of my desperate situation and life situation... and after this and that ugly fish had swallowed the bait... these fish should be nailed. All my enemies should hopefully be nailed if I just allowed myself to forget all about, for the time being, my dangerous knowledge of how to be an agent for DBIA. Finally, all my memories disappeared. I was then in a dream-like situation driven home to my mother in a taxi cab. I also in a dream-like way went to my mother's apartment, and in a dreamlike way I entered my mother's apartment, and then in a dreamlike way I said: 'Good night.'

Chapter 5:

A GENIUS OR NOBODY IS REELING OUT OF THE UNIVERSITY

I suddenly awoke early in the morning with a strange feeling that my brain was somehow washed out and because of this, I wondered if I had forgotten something about some relations outside BAD Cupboard Department and Monte Fresco University. Hmm, strange... I felt I had forgotten something but I couldn't remember what it was... although I tried. Gosh! Why should I always run into confusion? I now looked around and I found out that I was in my mother's apartment. My mother named Astrid looked worried... when she looked at me... but I soon recovered... after I had smashed a chair in pure desperation... because I felt nothing was changed as far as my miserable situation was concerned.

Anyway, I now as usual went back to my "jail" named BAD Cupboard Department, and soon after I had arrived... I was talking to one of the university teachers, Dr. Samuelson. I went into his office room, and there I now learned he had been appointed acting professor for Paul Frenkner.

I said: 'I am very interested in responsible accounting. Otherwise, I must say... that I feel this research program of courses... this research program consists of a lot of disparate courses leading to no real competence... This doesn't get me anywhere! Well, I don't like to make the same research as some kind of Donald Duck... just because this research program is a complete disaster. A lot of courses and no plan. All this is nothing but terror, terror, and more terror! I am not happy with this research program!

However, your course about responsibility accounting seems very interesting to me.'

Dr. Samuelson still showed a neutral attitude, but now the attitude had become slightly worried which was shown in one corner of the mouth. Dr. Samuelson had somehow changed his attitude as if he wanted to forget about his course, but then he said: 'You are interested, hmm? Your attitude tells me that you also are aware of something, eh?'

I answered: 'Yes, Christ! I am interested in possible wrongdoings or no-doings at BAD Department!'

Dr. Samuelson mumbled something which was supposed to be some kind of agreement, but with a whole list of silent buts, silent reservations, and then he in a very silent way looked into his new drawer for a course specification. Hmm, perhaps some part of the course should... also remain in silence.

Dr. Samuelson: 'Hmm, the course specification... Here it is.'

I now looked through the different contents and then I said: 'Yes, the budgetary process and accounting and accountability, and I am interested in... in what is going on here...'

Dr. Samuelson: 'This university consists not only of BAD Department.'

I asked: 'If I sometimes... during this course period... will catch some opportunity... to talk with that fellow who is responsible for the whole overall budgetary process of this university...?'

Dr, Samuelson: 'Herr Fürstenbach... is the name.'

I said: 'Okay, Herr Fürstenbach... and if I could ask him some questions... perhaps of this Monte Fresco University, a budgetary process which he is accountable for...?'

Dr. Samuelson took up a laconic attitude in tone, voice, expression, and the like when he now said: 'Yes, I hope Herr Fürstenbach will tell you something. I will try to arrange a meeting for you.'

I now during the course wrote down a number of questions about the budgetary process, but when I finally met and asked Herr Fürstenbach if he did take some special considerations when he was performing the budgetary process... then I was thinking of this judicial murder of my rights... but Herr Fürstenbach just pretend he hadn't understood what I aiming at.

I tried again, asking: 'Maybe I have to express myself better? Do you, Mr. Fürstenbach, take advantage of certain situations to improve university interests related to the budgetary process?'

Fürstenbach: 'Well, not if it means bad morals. Of course!'

I now thought in silence: 'Strange, Mr.Toby at BAD Department doesn't know anything about such a situation either. At the lowest level, they don't know anything. At the middle level, you don't seem to know anything either, Herr Fürstenbach. What about the top level, the chairman Mr. Lovebeer?'

Herr Fürstenbach: 'Now, do you have something to add?'

I said: 'Hmm, you Herr Fürstenbach, and Mr. Toby at BAD

Department... you must at least have informed Herr Lovebeer, the chairman of the university board... about some/my situation and...?'

Fürstenbach: 'Whatever situation you are referring to... this "The Monte Fresco University" will only benefit from having you here within the framework of your kind of employment, and I have heard that you should be some kind of extra resource of labor being added to the normal labor force.'

I replied: 'Yes, I feel this whole situation of mine... at this university... is indeed... very extra!?'

Fürstenbach now took on a very determined bureaucratic attitude when saying: 'Yes, your salary accounts have been established for you at the Stockholm County Council. We, at this university, have nothing to do with those accounts. Well, I think time is running out. I hope I have been to some use.'

Perplexed, I answered: 'Yes, thanks. I then in silence added: 'Now, I know the limitation of civilized interviews in certain interview situations.'

When I was out of sight, I silently said to myself: 'Sunday school interviews and school talk! who uses whom? That's one question! No one seems to be accountable to any written law in force, to any decision taken, to any honest and upright auditor! this very auditor from the Swedish National Audit Office named Lee SaLasso, now obviously has learned when to close his eyes and when to allow certain people to override & underride the very principle of "rule by law". I feel upset, but I also feel... hopelessness.'

A number of days later, one morning... I was driving from my big cabin or small house to a parking lot nearby the subway station. Yes, I intended and was also going to this pompous Stockholm university named Monte Fresco University by subway I parked my car there, as I had done some times before. Later in the evening, when I should go back to my big cabin or small house then I found my car gone. I phoned the police. A few days later, then the police phoned me back and told me that my car had been found. Yes, it was found quite near my parking lot, some blocks away. I now interpreted the situation as some kind of warning... that I shouldn't go around and ask questions and do my own thinking. Hmm, when it was too expensive and inconvenient to live at some Divine Island, then I stayed at my mother's apartment.

Now, this situation along with other situations was still damn fresh in my memory when I waited for an opportunity to do some talking with a female jurist... Mrs. Lawdotted. A woman whom I first met in the kitchen of BAD Cupboard Department where she made coffee and bread... and now when we first met, we were alone... I and this Mrs. Lawdotted... quite late in the evening. Hmm, for some reason the office room of Mrs. Lawdotted was located between "my" office room at BAD Department and some department for media research. Yes, the office room of Mrs. Lawdotted was located between my office room and some department for media research. A department that recently had become a neighbor to BAD Department. Again, the office room of Mrs. Lawdotted was located between the BAD Department and this Department of media research. I now talked to this Mrs. Lawdotted about the strange different situations that

I had to face, at BAD Department. When I then also asked Mrs. Lawdotted if the Swedish legal system really was reliable, then she didn't answer hmm, no answer is also some kind of answer.

I now also waited for an opportunity to talk to a man named Mr. Presston, and he did also occupy an office room in the same corner where I stayed. He was doing media research. Hmm, when Mr. Presston went by or passed by my office room and said hello through the open office door... then I went to his office room. Hmm, he didn't answer when I asked him if a journalist like Carrol Foge was reliable... a journalist working for Wasp Express this Mr. Presston look like a nice guy who smiled now and then and who scratched his head, not his non-existing hair being not covered by any wig, now and then. Yes, Mr. Presston seemed to be a nice guy... but appearances may sometimes be deceptive. Now, what kind of media research did this Mr. Presston really carry out, and for what purpose? Anyway, why did the Media Research Centre choose their premises next door to "my" very BAD Cupboard Department? Hmm, maybe the question is the answer. I thought I was under observation or probation. Probably, the Swedish Media should me... who they indirectly should pay attention to, and if a suitable opportunity should appear for Swedish Media to fire some for my compromising allusions, then so be it.

I now realized that I had experienced at least two indicators. The first indicator was the behavior of Mrs. Lawdotted when I asked if the observance of Swedish laws could be trusted. The other indicator was the behavior of Mr. Presston when I asked if the Swedish Press could be trusted. I realized or felt that some kind of strange dissenters... some people like myself, can't trust the Swedish Law...

nor the Press! Yes, the performances of Mrs. Lawdotted and Mr. Presston were the two indicators that made me decide not to trust the mass media or the legal system. Simple people like me, myself, and I... can only tremble and cherish a flickering hope, and I stress hope, that media people and law people will carry out their duties. I became no doubt very depressed when I could see representatives of law and media just stay around and occupy some part of the same corridor as I... and do nothing at all while I and my future were strangled by a rope named judicial murder. Doom's Day! Decisions taken and laws in force are not anything you just neglect and ignore, I thought, but obviously, Swedish authorities were of an opinion different than mine. Media and Law! Where are you!?

There had once also been another visitor at Cupboard Department, Pickodolly Binocular from Baltimore... who was and is president of a health consultant firm dealing with abuse problems and in so doing she was and is connected to the Washington administration. President Pickodolly Binocular sure knew and knows a lot about social dropouts. Hmm, I suspected she was informed about my situation. Hmm, experts on law, experts on Media, experts on those people who were dropouts of society... Yes, many were those individuals who observed the Skeleton phenomenon... but they never talked to me about it, not in plain language. Hmm, maybe I should have done it, instead... when Pickodolly asked me if I should visit the USA.

Yes, experts of law, media, and social problems were passing by my humble self, me always standing in solitude... in a desert of bureaucracy and corridors! I felt that the shy truth was locked and sealed. In my isolated solitude, I finally shouted: 'What's on!? What's on!? The experts were smiling, and didn't answer... and this they did and didn't do from a superior position. They had fine titles and they could perhaps destroy both my self-confidence and my reputation.'

Yes, one may wonder what's on... when I by chance, perhaps, overheard something in the BAD Coffee room/corridor... Professor Paul Frenkner happened to mention to somebody that some of my cousins had phoned and yelled and barked... some of my Marklund cousins, and this they had done and never said anything to me!

Sometime later... then I am sitting in the so-called EDP laboratory. From there I was calling Dr. Nichols, the EDP specialist. He was out, but then I vaulted two stairways and walked into his office room for not the first tie, and there my falcon eyes finally found something interesting, a hidden black notebook. Hmm, red Tavaritj Alexandrov, a Russian specialist in operation analysis... who as the candidate is to be guided by Dr. Nichols, his tutor. Hmm, Of course, it is ridiculous to jump to conclusions, but... Hmm, not too long time ago this Dr. Nichols in a very unexpected way was again appointed to acting professor in Helsinki, the capital of Finland, a country tied up to the Soviet Union... by very special war-related trade agreements. Oh boy!!

Time was passing, and I was still writing about different disabilities, and finally, I was going to hold a lecture about disability matters, but there was stormy weather. No one seemed to like this idea at BAD Cupboard Department... seemed to want the Skeleton out of the Cupboard. I was nevertheless holding that lecture in front of a really big audience consisting of only four people where I talked about functional problems related to human beings. The audience, about four people, did perhaps know more than I did... but they didn't talk too much. I had run into a ridiculous situation, again. However... why did they refuse to talk to me. Oh, some faces of stone... who didn't present themselves. They could have offered me some contacts with the so-called Swedish handicap movement. They did not.

Later, a British freelance university teacher named Knot Wales showed up. Once again, there was stormy weather and hard feelings... when I should perform a lecture.

When I anyway was going to meet that British lecturer and his audience to prove myself, giving a small lecture on communication and disability problems... then I could see the frightful appearance of this Christ Middler turning up in the doorway.

Perfect Christ Middler who knew that the lecture was to take place at ten o'clock had now decided that I should... just at ten o'clock... handle some urgent and pressing invoices. It was a fact that this university administration was working that slowly that delivery companies discussed a special time limit for invoices sent to this Monte Fresco University! That I had heard.

I looked at Christ Middler and then I told this Christ Middler that those invoices could wait for at least two hours. I had been strolling around for months without being used in a proper way as a head of labor or employee so why should that Christ Middler turn up right now? I could have handled those invoices weeks ago if asked. This perfect Christ Middler now however decided and demanded some work with those invoices, instantly. Did he do this out of pure cussedness just to prevent me from delivering my lecture? No, he wasn't that kind of fellow. There was an ulterior motive somewhere, Hmm, but why?

That hypocrite and socialist or Social Democrat named Christ Middler ought to admit that the rules of staff management are both shifting and unclear, I thought. Well, obviously this is perfect of the BAD Department, Christ Middler... tried by all means to prevent me, the Skeleton, to get out of the Cupboard. Well, the cupboard was now the office room of Shyburger who now was in Africa, or should be. Oh, I was looking at Christ Middlerwho was standing in the doorway and represented some interests who wanted that I should be reduced to a nobody and if I was nobody, then I should remain a nobody a Cupboard!

Well, obviously Christ Middler wanted to withdraw any meaningful work task from my hands, even a temporary one, and if and when I as now in this way took my own initiatives he, Christ Middler, could try to prevent me from carrying out my intentions... Yes, Christ Middler could stop me by giving me some temporary work tasks during certain particular hours. Yeah, some people just should not be allowed to make any progress as employees, get new contacts, or whatever! Now, all this made me angry! Gosh! Where was that Swedish work therapy of solidarity to be found?

This Christ Middler obviously never wanted it to be known that I maybe had some qualities that so over. Was that this ugly purpose?

Ugly purpose... Hmm, but why?

I now looked at this Christ Middler and then I said: 'I don't care. I'm going to my lecture whether you want it or not.'

Christ Middler then placed himself in the doorway telling me that he couldn't allow me to perform my lecture.

I said: 'Oh. Christ! I remember when George Wallace, that Dixieracist, was standing in front of an entrance door to a university trying, trying to prevent black people to take part in the knowledge of science. You seem to like Wallace style, way back in the late fifties and early sixties!'

Christ Middler: 'No politics! I am just doing my job!'

I said; 'Well, Wallace had also a job to do.'

Christ Middler: 'You can't compare!'

I said: 'Yes, why doesn't a Swedish left-wing do goodie like you Christ Middler shake hands with people like Wallace? People with the same attitude to low-ranking minorities and individuals should stick together and polish their boots. Stalin and Hitler and Pol Pot should also stick together. Now, what shall I say to that honorable? British egghead, knot Wales? He is expecting me now. Why can't I be allowed to prove myself? Why do you have to change the policy of staff management from one time to another? I am just asking, you socialist angel of very strange nature!'

Christ Middler: 'No comments.'

I said: 'By the way, get out of my way.'

Christ Middler didn't.

Now a boxing match began between two merciless antagonists and I just wanted to defend my rights and thereby myself. I and Middler now put our head gears on... just as the first gong was calling. A cap like me had to defend himself against a hat like Christ Middler.

In the first round now taking place; I tried to push this hat Christ Middler away from the door. Christ Middler, however, goes to counterattack in a defensive way.

In the second round, a tough cap like me was firing off a number of smack taps just to warm up a little.

In the third round, Christ Middler obviously had succeeded in provoking me to use physical violence, just a little, Now, he doesn't defend himself anymore, and hey presto, a ”hired” “objective“ university teacher appeared, shouting, “break it”... I certainly disapproved of this dishonest break of a very honest boxing match being an honest expression of how the little guy uses the noble art self-defense when Perfect and criminal fellow traveler being run by ulterior motives try to harass me, but I stopped.

Now Christ Middler could run away and tell tales to a likewise “objective” medical doctor who could in some “objective” way confirm something... something confirms which did suit Christ Middler already thought he was dead! Oh, that man had a vivid imagination around the concept of martyrdom! Oh, Christ!

Now, I finally went to Know Wales and a set of “lectures”. I was bloody cool if I may say so. I held my lecture talking about disability aspects being related to some consumer communication process as if nothing had happened. In my model of consumer communication... there I pressed in a number of factors like audience section, filters in media, symbols, thoughts, and feedback. The honorable British egghead Knot Wales was pleased and so was the audience. However, when I was back at Cupboard Department or BAD Department two policemen rose their caps or maybe they didn't but they told me to follow them to the police station.

I told those two policemen that I was not guilty, guilty was Christ Middler.

The polite policemen "realized" that Middler, of course, was right and off we went... to the police station, named "Three Fasces". I tried to tell those two policemen that they had got the wrong guy, but no one of those two policemen did take an interest. Obviously... I wasn't allowed to exercise the noble art of self-defense against a criminal staff management of cruel oppression which destroyed my reputation Anyway, at the police station this nutty boxing match between me and Christ Middler was registered.

The police doctor was a certain Dr. Beirot... Dr. Beirot is a man of heavy authority, I thought. He was now going to cross-examine me.. about the boxing match. Dr. Beirot blew up himself and said full of boiling indignation: 'Don't you understand that you can't use physical violence against a most honorable socialist, well established as a part of the famous Swedish World Conscience, which could be linked to some solidarity business!'

I scratched my head and answered: 'Oh, solidarity business? Yes, I thought he was business-minded in some tricky way. Yes, he is Christ Middler and should be teaching profit maximizing. Well, he does. Sir, I want to say that this socialist Middler... he provoked me as if he was a man like that racist George Wallace. Oh boy! What a terrible man that was! Middler, provoked me all the time! The idea was that I shouldn't be able to make any progress at all! I have been exposed to psychological torture! Sooner or later one of his provocations must be succeeded... Sir!'

Dr. Beirot: 'Bah! That Mr. Middler has told me that you are unstable and neurotic and sick. He said that you are not responsible for your actions.'

I said: 'No, I am responsible for my actions. However, if I am unstable, then the problem has been created by poor staff management, but okay... I have a problem. Yes, and Christ Middler really does like to create conditions for that my problem to remain. Problem maintenance! Maybe, Christ also wants to prove that I am a madcap, a madcap who is telling me not responsible for "his=my" actions.'

Dr. Beirot: 'Hmm, I guess you have to be replaced somehow at that Monte Fresco University. Well, we will see what comes out of this.

I now walked out to dubious freedom.

For the first time, after six years that staff manager at Monte Fresco University, Hardy Viceman, seemed to take some notice of my existence. I was called up... to visit this fellow in his office room.

Hardy Viceman twirled his thumbs and then he said: 'You have some defect in your head here, haven't you? Do you know what kind of person you are? You are a burglar. We have found you ransacking the office rooms in the BAD Department in the middle of the night. Suspicious behavior, isn't it? You have used physical violence against a most honorable specialist, Mr. Middler. You don't bring back the books you have borrowed from the library, you don't work as honest people do I am deeply shocked!'

I answered: 'Let's in a very scientific way examine the law of cause and effect.'

I now could hear Hardy Viceman sigh and he sank down behind his desk. Only his front head and pair of so-called terrified pair of eyes were visible to me.

I continued saying: 'That's true! I was found in the office room of Hans Thompson, but I wanted to go through his papers. I felt he spied on me! I also hoped for an explanation of why I was and am treated the way I was and am treated! For instance, why Christ Middler had to stay in the doorway when I should perform a small lecture!? He had banned me from work and then doorway and asked me to perform work... of handling some invoices exactly during that time while my small lecture should be performed! Then I should be frozen out of work again, although I wanted to work! Of course, I got angry! Furthermore, the books I borrowed... I borrowed those books for Sunway Sweetiepie and Buddy Stone... and I am sorry they haven't returned those books to the library. Hmm, they seem to have forgotten that they once asked me to borrow the books for them... and now the librarians do blame me because the only fact those librarians know about is... that I borrowed the books... and now I... therefore, have become some scapegoat!... Hmm, many an evil cause and some unfair effect... that is what this, what shall I call it... "Management System of Distracted Subsidized Low Wage Labor", has produced!

Now... the phone was ringing and Hardy Viceman had no more time for me I was fast out of that office room Hardy Viceman. When Assisting Professor Boo shyburger for only a while... was back from Africa/Tanzania... then he gave me a hint... that his wife should be glad to see me... as a sexy playmate. Obviously, I could be useful in a sexy way. Obviously, my fate was of poor appearance... and I wasn't Man enough to fight that dishonorable fate of mine... Obviously, I wasn't worthy of being a serious candidate for the doctorate at this fine BAD Department according to Assisting Professor Boo Shyburger. Obviously, Assisting Professor Boo Shyburger was worthy of this BAD Department! Well, I pity those candidates who trust that man Boo Shyburger with his criminal attitude. Yes, indeed... pompous Assisting Professor Boo Shyburger. Hmm, this Assisting Professor Boo Shyburger also told me that I had "no keys to start up a scientific project" and he also told me that I had entered that BAD Department in the wrong way referring to that relief work of mine or "funny" employment of mine. Well, I slowly then concluded that when there is no space for respect and cooperation... then out of that, may very well, and hopefully... a conflict rise. I wanted to die fighting rather than living in slavery or serfhood.

I then went to "The Corporation Health Care". There I told a nurse what I had been through.

The nurse told me: 'You have to realize that you are mean to yourself!'

I answered: 'I feel someone else is mean towards me.'

The discussion did lead to nothing and I realized that I, somehow...

had fallen victim to a bogus system.

I had made myself impossible, but nevertheless, I was offered a temporary office room at the "Department of Housing Maintenance" of Monte Fresco University... as some kind of replaced problem child, I believe. Hmm, in the coffee room at that department, I could overhear an old "gentleman " saying: 'Those people working for "The Corporation Health Care" should be left alone in "peace and quiet".

I was very disillusioned!

Although I had an office room at the "Department of Housing Maintenance"... I was now at my own request... working at "The Academy of Social Studies". Yes, I got temporary work there being assigned to a project group. I was working for a certain Mrs. Putman who was working for a woman... Dr. Peterson, being the project leader. Yes, I was now enrolled in this project group, a project group that was assigned to work tasks focusing on the evaluation of the anticipated effects of certain proposed laws related to certain social problems. Yes, the project was dealing with an anticipated evaluation of certain legislation regarding social service.

Now, the project leader was named Dr. Ulla Peterson and she had to answer for and present her results to... a certain Professor Control. A professor who probably always wanted and wants total control over the so-called sub-normal population of human beings in this country, Sweden. Hmm, and his colleague professor at "The Academy of Social Studies" was named Professor Jansson.

I was doing my duty when I now was dragging out a lot of statistics about five different urban districts. I did study variables like incomes, consumer price indexes, housing, commuting between those urban districts, trade, education, family size, age, sex, unemployment, social welfare, and taxation number of inhabitants... Yes, I was studying those variables which all were shifting in time in those five different urban districts.

Now, I did some systematizing and presented my figures to Mrs. Putman, Dr. Peterson, and Professor Control.

Parallelly... with my dragging and systematizing of figures... there were some very deep interviews carried out by those other people working on this project led by Dr. Peterson, this project deals with the evaluation of anticipated effects of some proposed national Swedish legislation of social service. Hmm, social and socio-economical experimental models foregoing social and socio-economical legislation?

I who had been working with statistics here in Sweden of course realized... that in Sweden there were possibilities to link individuals to the statistics. Not to mention longitudinal time studies which may include different information about the kinder garden, schools, first jobs, family, skills, social career, sickness, pensions, crimes and drug abuse, medicals, and death. Well, in Sweden there's a personal identification number linked to every individual on many an ADP-based file. Hmm, many thousands of such files, and then there are compilation programs. Hmm, I now thought of how social control of different segments of the Swedish population, especially social control of the subnormal Swedish population of human beings... could be combined with this proposed social legislation.

Of course, I wondered if I, myself, could be registered in such an evil national overall system of social control/"diagnosis" and pussification/"therapy"... I myself am most likely a member of the subnormal Swedish population of "human?" individuals. Well, all information doesn't need to object to EDP or ADP. Information related to dissenters like me can also be off the record... in a loose-leaf binder. Yes, I was also bugged and controlled and as a dissenter also recorded on a so-called; X-file. Well, I had no solid evidence, but I could feel it in my bones.

Who knows what kind of more information there is around regarding my humble self, I now thought. For a while; I now began to think along those lines.

I now visited a Feminist organization a few times... and after one of those times I as usual went underground looking for the subway train... I was wondering ... about social control. All those files! Hmm, I thought the press might be an accomplice.

Wondering about those issues I was at a subway station and bought a female monthly magazine named Hertha or was it "Female Justice"... and this magazine was dealing with topics like male chauvinism and oppression. Gosh! I was a thunderstick! This female magazine described the same oppression... that I myself had been exposed to! This paper described oppression... obviously now and then and more or less in a systematic way, I thought. Yes, this female magazine described something like staff management oppression & harassment... all very clearly and concisely!

The next day when I was back at "The Academy of Social Studies"...

then I there gave a copy of this article on male oppression techniques being printed in that monthly feminist magazine named Herta... to Dr. Peterson and to Dr. Putman. They received a copy of the article and said, "Thank you". However, they refused in practice to discuss that controversial magazine article, with me. Yes, at "The Academy of Social Studies"... there in the project group... they were very careful not to discuss the controversial subject of how to exercise techniques and methods of social control, with me. Hmm, I bet, however, that Dr. Ulla Peterson and Dr. Anne Putman discussed this magazine article and the subject of social control with other people, people from the Swedish establishment, but not with me. Yes, even Dr. Putman and Dr. Ulla Peterson took part in the conspiracy against me because they probably had to.

I had found an invisible class barrier between me and Dr. Putman & Dr. Peterson. They were better people doing good things but I being white trash just had to do as good as I could. Yes, I discovered the invisible class barrier where the discussion stops.

Oh boy! I was locked out from further work again. I limped to Wennergen Center. I applied for the money for a fishy research project, but being around that Centre I finally could overhear that they didn't want someone who was dragged into "politics". Yes, maybe I was dragged into a political game... Well, if I was a manipulated ignorant peasant, being all dragged into and part of a political game, then I had to draw certain conclusions.

I now finally figured out that I had to perform my own private investigation to get proper results... and I had to dig where I stood... looking at my own situation. In so doing; I realized that I... in this rotten and corrupt Swedish Welfare State... couldn't and shouldn't rely on any organization, any group, or any individual.

Sometime later I once was invited to the house of Dr. Anne Putman and her husband, Peter Puide Putman. This Mr. Putman was a refugee from those Baltic nations. He was in the advertising business... and he wrote novels as well.

A lot of rumors were circulating in the air and therefore and because of some kind of desperation I tried the idea of going to a spectacular Off shore fair in Gothenburg. There, I noticed the exhibition case of tet company Cow Safe. Cow Safe was an extraordinary new company that was selling or renting out offshore constructions like apartment platforms. Oh, those contracts. Hmm, who did he, this Christ Ericson who owned Cow Safe AB, turn to if he got problems with corrosion, etc? Beckers AB, I supposed... and this was of some interest to me, since the financial manager working in that company was listening to the name Max Endre... also being that Max Endre who some hours a week worked as a university teacher at BAD Cupboard Department, the fellow who I once ran into at BAD Department.

I did now continue looking, being at this Offshore fair in Gothenburg, and I suddenly looked at the exhibition case of Johnson Traders. Johnson Traders was a company connected to the owner Antonia Axe Johnson, a woman who was and is trading not only in oil and coal but also in "Electronic Data Processing" including both software and hardware... Hmm, I wondered if that woman Antonia Axe Johnson perhaps also did consider the slurry problem, that problem which is dealing with how to convert coal into oil. Yes, what a wonderful problem! I was in a green mood. I took it for granted that the owner of Johnson Traders... herself... that Antonia Axe Johnson... was completely caught by a straight fascination with this slurry problem.

Hmm, energy costs and oil drilling offshore is expensive, I thought maybe the British Union boys... Scargill and his tough coal miners... do have an answer to the slurry problem, I also thought. I provided myself with leaflets, standing at that exhibition case of Johnson Traders. Then, I went to hear some talk shoes regarding the offshore industry.

When I was back at Monte Fresco University and "The Academy of Social Studies"... then a publisher from Wasp Express named Dan Bonnier showed up. I talked with this Dan Bonnier about research statistics. How energy taxes can influence the use of different energy sources. I recalled this journalist Carrol Foge who worked for Wasp Express, and who had passed through a big energy course... for Guran Edby.

Dan Bonnier expressed his point of view saying: 'The Swedish Government isn't that sophisticated. They just want to vacuum clean all money there is to get, in order to finance a degenerated public sector.'

I now added: 'Do you want to check my thesis about it?'

Dan Bonnier: 'Sure, but I think you should get in touch with Mr. Teddy Jeansen and his STC Venture.'

I muttered to myself very silently: 'Hmm, Teddy Jeansen...? I try to remember him. I will check with him later when I know more.

Hmm, STC stands for Scandinavian Trading Centre. STC Venture. Hmm, energy costs!?'

I in this situation also wrote down certain new thesis addressed to that very important but dangerous businesswoman named Antonia Axe Johnson. I wrote to her and then I phoned her. Someone played the drunken sailor on the phone. Strange! Was it that dangerous "black lady" Antonia Axe Johnson? Well, I wanted to talk about coal with Antonia Axe Johnson because the coal and energy trade constituted some link to some oily other trade which was perhaps as black as coal in some slurry-like way, but this I didn't say or wrote... Yes, someone just made fun of me when I called Antonia Axe Johnson... but I'll get the last laugh, I thought.

I later phoned the secretary of Antonia Johnson... I then wrote a letter, and I finally got a written answer, an answer which to me was the wrong kind of answer. This Antonia obviously really didn't need me! To my surprise; I was not surprised! Hmm, I realized that I had made myself ridiculous. After this; I never did dare to speak about coal! I blushed. Coal! I suddenly recovered from my disease of self-criticism. Hmm, if people just knew how many possible or impossible relations there are to a piece of coal! Scargill knew when he mobilized his coal workers in Barnsley. Anyway, I sure also was acting seriously, but no one understood my position and my strategy! Therefore, I was made ridiculous! I was desperate and considered not to be rational but childish and I was laughed at just as some circles of people laughed at the coal miners being in a desperate situation. However, no one, not even Antonia Axe Johnson should be allowed to laugh away my serious work as a detective! I obviously had to prove myself or be damned and this being the case I should prove myself in a case I should prove myself in a merciless way. I was angry! hmm, spoiled cruel upper-class people and Solemn Gown of criminal Scientific nature and Greedy Town... Names! I was angry! I am still angry!

I now phoned "The Distracted Subsidized Low-Wage Labor-Exchange", that special sub-organization that was dealing with unattractive labor... and now answered did... and this Mrs. Kickpawn who once had helped me to find this "work-relief employment which should include some work therapy" at a certain BAD Department which for me=Skeleton became a Cupboard Department. Yes, Mrs. Kickpawn answered, and this Mrs. Mittler Kickpawn now just giggled when I told her my name. Hmm, the Swedish welfare system and serious commitments and some high degree of pretense. Well, Mrs. Kickpawn just giggled when I told her that things were not the way they ought to be. Yes, some people didn't take a commitment with me... seriously I was a humiliated beggar.

When I hung up the phone, some time passed and then I very slowly and finally realized that those relief works obviously shouldn't get too attractive! While I now still was holding that Swedish relief work... I sure felt that I had to do some thinking. After all... I was now almost destroyed by that relief work of mine. My whole reputation and also my chances at any labor market... were or had now been destroyed. I somehow in this situation felt that I had reached a point of no return and now I had either to pull up my "house piles" and move to other hunting grounds or die or just fade away into some Skeleton appearing position. Anyway, I felt it was necessary for me to study how solid the Swedish welfare system really was and if there were some welfare sharks with ulterior motives swimming around... and I now finally felt that I was on my way to reaching the bottom of his complex matter which a relief work obviously sometimes could prove to be. Me and science! Hmm, difficult when big criminal actors are physical games! Empirical research the hard way! How and I not suffered! Yes, and now I felt I had sacrificed everything for my Skeleton like case study! A case study; where I and my problem with blacklisting were related to the ramifications of extortion. Yes, my Skeleton is like a case study, with an outlook from a cupboard... It was too much! It was too much! I now realized I had to fire myself! Kick me in the ass so to speak! Destiny had shown to me, that whatever way I choose to walk... this way should be a way of no return! I had to go to the bottom of some matters! A man or a mouse got to do what a man or mouse has to do! Hmm, I just hoped that I had collected enough empirical data! Hmm, observation by participation.

Now, I had got a new office room where I was sitting... a new office room at "The Department of Housing Maintenance"... but now I also had decided that I should quit my strange employment at Monte Fresco University and then shortly after that announcement... I was advised by those people at "The Department of Housing Maintenance" to apply for a passport, but for what reason...?

Chapter 6: UNEMPLOYED

I now phoned Professor Sunway Sweetiepie in this difficult situation of mine. Why? Because... I instinctively felt that she was a decent and considerate woman with human feelings. However, she didn't want to see me. I assumed she wasn't allowed to. There was also perhaps someone who tapped the wires, who knows? Hmm, I believe some Swedish policeman and then I like and like Sunway Sweetiepie and believed and still believes that she someday will and she certainly should give me her explanation of how things had been handled at "my" very BAD Cupboard Department but her relation to the big truth may not be all that splendid, I am afraid. The staff management at Monte Fresco University didn't want to do anything... except they expressed their wish that I should stay "employed", as usual! Well, some women are some kind of assistants related to the staff management of Monte Fresco University, she first suggested that I should go to high-life parties, obviously with bandaged eyes", and when I turned down that suggestion, then she finally became really desperate and suggested some employment at a company named Trelleborg AB, but why should a private company now want to hire me if not for some ulterior motive... so I also turned that down... because I didn't trust this whole staff management of Monte Fresco University. I now anyway felt that I had it... and therefore I decided, quite automatically decided, to slip out of that Monte Fresco University as smoothly and painlessly as possible. Now, I had to state that all which I ever had got or should get from this Monte Fresco University was a totally worthless letter of reference from this dubious Scotchman Hunter Mabon, plus a very brutal and long-lasting lesson in black pedagogy which did shake me up, and made me tremble... and then got me stirred. Well, that was a well-shaken starting point to get stirred for a fellow like me who is looking for some kind of right opportunity.

I now had to put an end to this sojourn at Monte Fresco University and therefore I now collected my books and put them in my car. While I did that a couple of times... I also had to pass that very BAD Cupboard Department... where I in some garbage can happened to find some strange dented doctoral hat on my head... and I also succeeded to pull up my right sock, but I failed when I tried to do the same thing with my left sock.

Suddenly... over the garbage can, something raised over the garbage can... and that something was the Spirit of Platon, and the spirit hissed: 'Has there ever been a greater foolosophere than this one?'

Now, behind the Spirit of Platon, the Spirit of Shakespeare... raised, and this spirit said: 'Yes, that foolosopher, he sure has some special insight and understanding about things in life, haw... the foolosophers usually do.'

I now, carrying a big number of books, limped or hopped towards the exit of this Monte Fresco University. Before, I passed the Exit; I, however, heard this phrase from an invisible crowd in a way cruel smiling university people, a phrase being whispered: 'He has or can blame nobody but himself, for his own failure!'

Now, being in a strange mood, I could drive to my big cabin or small house with all my books. Yes, I then also drove to the Divine Island... where my big cabin or small house... was situated.

When I then went back to my mother and it was in June 1983... then I noticed that this now assisting professor from BAD Department... that assisting professor who was named Boo Shyburger... he had fixed himself an apartment situated at the other side of the street vis-a-vis my mother's apartment. Hmm, obviously this... assisting professor who now was employed as some kind of assitance worker in Africa for the time being, this Boo Shyburger, obviously he wasn't always to be found in Dar-Es-Salam and Tanzania where he should spend most of his time... and hopefully he shouldn't only spend time and tax money there, but also achieve some useful results. Hmm that new apartment of Shyburger... should he compromise me more than spy on me or what? I could feel the smell of a rat. Hmm, I could see some guards with black sun glasses standing outside this Boo Shyburger's new apartment, so my conclusion was that it shouldn't be appropriate for me to visit that apartment, ever. Hmm, this new apartment of Shyburger... Conspicious! Hmm, this renting of an apartment by Boo Shyburger living/staying then quite close to my dwelling place of writing... was no coincidence... but instead it was cold calculated non-verbal calumny. Well, Boo Shyburger was/is most likely acting in immoral if not criminal agreement with other people and he should be brought into custody for interrogation. Hmm, criminal schemes and Boo Shyburger's participation. Hmm, I now finally had left this Monte Fresco University and I now was supposed to look for a job elsewhere. I hardly did. No luck!

Hard luck! I also sure noticed that I didn't receive this unemployment benefit because I did quit by so-called free choice. Oh, that free choice! Yes, a free choice only in a tricky formal sense! Yes, you do quit when you are banned from education and work... or bossed around, harrassed, etc, but of free choice? I also noticed that the union didn't do anything about all this! Was this not a member free fraud! The ST-union should at least have given me some information hints! This ST-union could also have tested my work capacity if they had wanted to defend my rights in negotiations my rights which "my" so-called ST-union didn't defend and therefore "my" ST-union did contribute to ignorant rumors being full of prejudices destroying my life. The Swedish ST-union had forgotten that concept of solidarity, and now they were fellow travellers in crime, and in "my" case more active than passive, showing some cynical calculating contempt to 100% and solidarity respect to 0%. No, there were no hints of explaining information from the union, there were no tests of my work capacity made by the union, there were no nothing services from the union... and therefore this Swedish ST-union was guilty of member fee fraud... when I didn't got my unemployment benefit! However, I believe some Swedish union people are clever to make excuses for their frauds! Hmm, still... the Swedish ST-union did also commit member fee fraud... when I didn't got my unemployment benefit! However, I believe some Swedish union people are clever to make excuses for their frauds! Hmm, still... the Swedish ST-union or TCO as a whole, must have got more than thirty coins of silver when they betrayed me... or got something of more value than thirty coins of silver when they carried out criminal negotiations.

I now decided to visit the Swedish Labor Exchange, and I should receive information service. I had to wait but finally I was... due to tele-communications... received by some kind of exchange officer named Kitty Grande who then informed me how I should transport myself to her office room. I did... The discussion could then be described as follows cut and dried.

I said: 'I want information about a game being played above my somewhat ignorant head... at my former work place. I there quitted some kind of strange relief work, but... I am still... in a so-called research program there.'

Kitty Grande: 'I will phone them. You may come back in two weeks.'

I was after two weeks back and then this secretary Kitty said: 'Your references were bad. We have heard those civil servants and university teachers responsible... at BAD Department and Monte Fresco University.'

I said: 'Oh, no names mentioned? These people jut tell lies!'

Kitty Grande: 'Where is that information you have got, information who you can use to prove your point of views against the authorities and experts and their excellent judgements. That information doesn't exist! Therefore, I have no trust in your wordings.'

I remarked: 'Yes, but I am the one who need information!'

Kitty Grande: 'About what?'

I replied: 'Phew! Why some people didn't follow the decisions and rules stipulated vis-a-vis me and also exercised discrimination against me at this Monte Fresco University, do you understand my double question!? Please, give me at least a hint!... why people at BAD Department have acted. Why was I employed at BAD Department... as some kind of waiter... where did nothing? Hmm, the Swedish waiter who waited for decisions correctly realized, ehh?'

Kitty Grande tried to be friendly and trustworthy when she said: 'Oh boy! Why don't you go to a psychiatrist!? I know a really good one. He is named Herr Rinnan. I think you should look him up. Here is a photo of him. He is a nice and understanding fellow who can offer a special kind of therapy just for people like you. Maybe our common friend Dr. Rihann can help you to specify your need for information? You can have confidence in Dr. Rihann, a Norwegian fellow who has worked with disciplined German therapists being ready to help you if the Swedish therapists can't. Hmm, therapy leading to heaven. You should be happy to be around here in Sweden, where you really can trust the authorities. Yes, Dr. Rihann can help you to identify or specify your need for information.'

I answered: 'I can't be more precise, since I have no information that has been stamped as secret, some information is stored in computer memory, but I can't find it because I do not know how this information is so secret that it is not registered at all. Give me a clue!'

Kittty Grande: 'I have no more time with chatterboxes. I have more important things to do. Fill out those blanks and be sure you are available for actors on the labor market anytime babe!'

I said: 'I can show you that those references which you have got from Monte Fresco University are false, I --------------------think I can prove that by passing a test... we could...'

Kitty Grande: 'We don't need to know anything more! Goodbye!'

I limped out through the office door of Kitty Grande and also did I pass some premises of the Labor Exchange and finally, I limped out through the front door of the whole Labor Exchange building. Yes, I was now out in the cold... standing on the street, looking at the "Labor Exchange" sign. Since no one had time, I also began to talk with the "labor exchange" sign. Gosh! I felt Sweden was a fascist country and a sanctuary for fascists when I now looked at Kitty Grande... The sign, however, didn't answer.

I said: 'Thank you sign... your answer was as good as that of a Swedish bureaucrat.'

I now remembered the last words of that secretary Kitty Grande: 'Make an appointment with the psychiatrist, Rinnan.' Hmm, I felt the secretary was trying to fool me into a trap. I did like the sign much better.

I now went home and then I went to bed. I fell asleep.

I met, in my sleep, Dr. Rinnan, a Norwegian Spirit of dark nature who like Kitty Grande had immigrated to Sweden, an ugly psychiatrist who told me: 'You begin to be too independent, Noman! You try in total freedom to create new theories and to sort out those complex problems you are a part of, but this is just compensation for your total lack of ideological instinct. Your theories are also divorced from reality because your theories aren't based on true facts, true facts which always are coming from that Swedish central government-run computer system, where the BIG TRUTH in letters and figures is always stored.'

I answered: 'What shall I believe, then... when I do not get any information!'

I now was bloody desperate.

The dream-like Dr. Rinnan: 'No, you don't get any information... and that's because you are sick! If you do not realize that you are sick then we certainly will force you to admit, to confess, that you are sick. You have to make the confession and go to the Swedish welfare state and all its experts. Also remember, that the United States is the enemy!' Hmm, I didn't miss the commanding of this psychiatrist when he played his part as a representative of the "good, enlightened, regulated, and authoritarian" Swedish Welfare State.

I felt the cruel help of this Swedish Welfare State when this Welfare State did and still does keep me short for reasons I don't understand.

Hmm, the dream went on and I asked: 'Why I never was allowed to do any work?... I said that nobody spoke to me, no one did notice me, and I was to be isolated and I was not to have any contact with other employees, inside and outside the university. Documents... documents that I didn't know of were produced about me in some arranged way... to suit some X-range-people. If not in theory I was in reality refused to do any "research work" at Monte Fresco University in spite of being accepted as a candidate for the doctorate. Because of all this, I now began to realize that I was swindled. Why should I hang on to Liers Express? Obviously, some, for me unknown and by me called... X-range-people... wanted to "kill?" me. That was what I thought. I now finally understood that I had to be careful and ignore all these Swedish authorities as much as possible! I now understood and still understand that someone was and still stand that someone was and still is prepared to destroy me or at least destroy my old Ego and kill my own personality and build up a new man ba Skeleton Man, who is more undead than alive, but I have never found out who that someone was or is, but he or she or they belonged to the X-range people. Well, talk about KKK hoods. Hmm, these privileges X-range people can and usually strike from far away in a superior position using the remote control and "remote control" without revealing their true identity and without showing their faces... and then they kick me around as a dubious form of entertainment.

Anyhow, the dream went on and I found myself out-frozen, controlled, and humiliated by the Swedish authorities. These authorities had done what they did to turn me into an easy-handled chessman. In this Swedish Welfare State, everybody should be a well-drilled chessman as some invisible and irresponsible Swedish social engineer now told me, in this dream of mine. If I don't become a chessman I will become an outlaw! That, I now thought. Hmm, such stubborn piss like me should obviously be cured the hard way by some "elegant" professionals, like Dr. Rinnan.

This is and was indeed a cruel play in some cruel sand pit where I had to wear green shorts all the time. I sighed: 'I am never to be confirmed.'

I now had a dream where I could see this secretary Kitty Grande.

A desperate mouse like me could now see how she called or phoned … now not Dr. Rinnan, but that director of Labor Exchange, named Allan Larson.

Kitty Grande now told Allan Larson something. She said: 'This strange Noman has gone now, and I don't think he will return to this place... Oh, I am sorry to say that I didn't succeed in getting him to that psychiatrist, Dr. Rinnan.'

I went on dreaming and now I could hear Allan Larson saying: 'I am sorry to hear this. This Noman should be available to the Labor market anytime. I am also sorry to hear that he won't visit this psychiatrist, Dr. Rinnan. Hmm, unfortunately, we can't force people like this Noman Skeleton to consult a psychiatrist like Dr. Rinnan... not yet... but we can always starve people like Noman until he becomes Skeleton and then surrender. Then, Noman has to put up with a fellow like Dr. Rinnan. Now, we have foreign eyes looking at us... Yes, and therefore we have to use only less hard indirect methods. Yes, if and when we want to enslave such a useful negotiation object and hostage-like object or chessman like Noman we have to be diplomatic! You see, Noman Skeleton might be guarded by foreign interests, sometimes being represented by foreign journalists for example... and therefore we can't use direct criminal methods when it comes to brainwashing and chemical enslavement in this Skeleton case, not yet.'

Chapter 7: MANIPULATIVE TALKS

Although I don't trust those damn politicians... I think it's better to hear of they have something to tell me, I finally thought. I looked at my telephone, being in that big cabin or small house of mine. I now phoned the Liberal Party. After some conversation those Liberals gave me a phone number... so I could speak to a soft wear consultant. His name was and still is Chip Fisher. We had a conversation and we both did agree that Information Technology was an interesting field of knowledge and an interesting science since I was curious about fields of applications this Chip Fisher finally admitted that this customer was to be found in the public sector, and then we decided to see each other at or in certain premises.

Sometime after the phone call... I began to get some vague idea why this man, Chip Fisher, was and is around in politics. He is around in politics to improve his own business, I told myself. This fact is at least a possibility, I thought. Wright or wrong my business... that he might think but never say, I also thought. At least; the thought wasn't unfamiliar with my way of thinking nowadays. Hmm, why did the Swedish Liberal Party bring two persons like me and Chip Fisher... together? Yes, that is a question.

When I finally met this Chip Fisher in the flesh at a political meeting, then I said: 'I have been kicked out of some strange BAD Department related to education and research and I have been kicked out without recommendations, and I know that this case of mine is a case of crime and discrimination, maybe even and very likely even a criminal plot. Laws and taken decisions have been violated.

This Liberal fellow who also was and maybe still is a software consultant and who was named Chip Fisher... he now said: 'I strongly do suggest that you join a special meeting that our political liberal party group will have. I think the root of all evils, is the union. Those union fellows allow themselves every kind of dirty trick in their thirst for power and influence.'

I asked: 'I suppose you are talking about those wages earner funds or in Swedish lingo... Swedish wage taker funds.'

Chip Fisher: 'Yes, that's right! Those funds have to be stopped! There is a meeting taking place where those wage taker funds will be discussed.'

I answered: 'Alright, I will show up, but I really don't see how this will solve my particular problems.'

Chip Fisher: 'Well, first you have to show some goodwill. Now, let's meet again at this so-called Hesinge commune-house... and when... Yes, let's meet again on the X;th, at 7:30 p.m.'

I drove to the meeting and I arrived twenty minutes before 7:30 p.m. Yes, I registered how those liberal politicians drop in one by one.

The meeting was performed by some kind of hired "political strategists". Yes, and their names were Mr. Smith and Mr. Wesson. Now, Mr. Wesson said: 'The Landwide Organization shortened LO, this nationwide Swedish umbrella-organization of many unions of blue-collar workers, that Giant Scoff-Scoff... does want to launch a special profit-dividing tax for private companies, and that special kind of tax shall be used to buy out the old owners who usually are normal shareholders, being natural persons or artificial persons.

First, however, there won't be any profit-dividing tax to collect for LO:s five wage-earner funds, if there won't be any company profits, and even if there will be company profits and even if there will be company profits then first the workers own pension funds have to be consolidated. When those pension funds have been consolidated and when their company profits... then the wage taker funds just grab 20% of the company profit! This is the profit tax. For that money, these Swedish wage taker funds then... will buy private companies, by buying blocks of shares.'

I asked: 'These union bosses do call this tax, and I mean this profit tax, but how can we talk about a profit tax? A tax isn't something you pay to central or local authorities, making it possible for those authorities to finance services that do meet collective needs like the judicature, the police force, public buildings, some social assistance, etc. You don't pay tax to some specific corporative like some normal union organizations making it possible for those unions to increase their power... unless these unions are labor corporations and as such corporative authorities... which then can increase their corporative power by financing their "buying and take-over" of private enterprise through a profit a wilful and deliberate attack against the corporative state of balance of power in Swedish society."

Mr. Smith: "Yes, I guess we just heard a quite correct definition of what that concept named tax is, and what it is not. Yes... and as you say the balance of that corporative power in Swedish society is jeopardized by these wage-taker funds, those wage-taker funds which are administered and managed by an organization, somewhat odd, an ordinary company or foundation, nor is it any kind of authority.'

I asked: 'So, what's the nature of those wage-taker funds then?'

Mr. Smith: 'Those wage-taker funds are not submitted to the principle of publicity rules like public authorities, nor are they submitted to the ordinary conditions of the market like private companies. Any comment?'

I remarked: 'Sure! You bet! This way of how to change the very meaning of the word tax... sounds to me like Orwell's so-called New Language. I guess this is an example of the Swedish Socialist kind of mental "Machtübernahme", going on since 1932/1933, eh? To say what I just said without even half a drop of irony felt quite natural... in that then-present and strongly present atmosphere of indignation and agitation. I added: 'Yes, as I said, a tax is something you charge people and corporations in order to finance activities of common interest. If that is the case, then you can also talk about a tax on profits. However, if specially organized interest groups like to line their own pockets and in this way increase their own power... living their own pockets for instance by arranging a special corporative tax going into the pockets of some corporations which could be some society of unions which then carry out speculation on the Stockholm Stock Exchange while the Social Democratic "minister of finance" stands beside them giving his union brothers inside information... then you can talk about how the word tax has gotten a quite new meaning!' I now suddenly reduced myself to silence while I was thinking of the Swedish unions as labor corporations, as Benito Mussolini would have put it... and as should also his ambassador in Stockholm has put it... that Italian ambassador who had a discussion with the Swedish Social Democratic prime minister Per Albin Hanson, in 1934... about the future of "The National Corporative Society".

Mr. Wesson: 'Well, these Swedish union tools named wage taker funds creating conditions for an even more strong centralized National Socialistic control of the Swedish society... this reality is hidden by some Swedish red "New Language"... Yes, that seems to be some general idea. Hmm, hopefully, I think this is just some hysterical last attempt by the Swedish "Rote Führer" Olof Palme... to carry out his socialist program before the tide turns.'

I mumbled: 'A beige führer who has turned too much towards red or rather rouge.'

Now, this friendly discussion went on for some time. Both Smith and Wesson mumbled something about... that something had to be done against the five big Swedish wage-taker funds, contemplated and planned. After those Swedish Liberals joined the Social Democratic Party. A remarkable suggestion! My political views hadn't been expressed in that direction and I thought that the different Swedish political parties should try hard to attract new members and voters. One guess of mine was that those Liberal chums were not interested to enroll likely losers like me as a new party member... nor did they like to enroll me or give me membership when I expected them to tell me what they could do for me before I became a member of the Liberal Party Another or more precisely or more precisely third guess of mine was that... maybe the Swedish Liberal Party had some agreement with the Swedish Social Democratic Party. Yes, perhaps, and probably there had been some political negotiations between Liberals and Social Democrats before those Liberals presented regarding my political membership. That was the impression I got talking to that foxy fellow Chip Fisher... as we were leaving the commune-house and walking to the parking lot... where we should jump into our cars. Yes, those Liberal chums were not interested to enroll likely losers like me for party membership... maybe they already regarded me as a 100% loser in all respects... so I thought as I now drove to my mother's apartment.

I phoned the Social Democratic Party. I was from now on not trying to live in my summer cabin now and then and I moved "back?" to and lived with my mother in her apartment one day I answered a request arriving through the maildrop... about membership in the Social Democratic Party... and a course was also offered.

I soon answered in writing: 'I am interested to join the course... and then later I might join the Social Democratic Party when I do know that I have got all things right.'

A few days later... I then phoned those Social Democrats, but then they just didn't seem to be interested. Did they want me to accept their red party and its red ideology with bandaged eyes? Maybe those Swedish Social Democrats were afraid of a sharp discussion? Yes, I guess those Social Democrats don't want to care about some enrollment of a certain new very curious inconvenient party member who may need their help... and I guess this kind of neglect was and is some kind of luxury that every strong and established political party can afford to pay. Well, Swedish party politics is probably anyway some kind of cartel arrangement, I now thought. Now, this is not good for common people who are interested in politics and want to join some established political party with for example seats in the Swedish Parliament, unless those common people are very cynical and calculating. Hmm, and why can't common Swedish people be cynical and calculating? I have in that respect no prejudices whatsoever. Yes, and sometimes those common Swedes are suspiciously confiding. Yes, I finally had left my big cabin or small house and I now more than stayed with my mother, named Astrid. I lived with her and I had no option I explained to her that I was shut out or excluded from the rest of this Swedish society. However, didn't I do some work on my big cabin or small house... and didn't get some help both from my mother and that always tricky carpenter being married to a certain cousin of mine? Yes, a second time that carpenter was around.

Many a rotten thing is going on in the kingdom of Sweden, I thought when I was driving to the US Embassy in Stockholm. When I now entered the Embassy I could hear that the staff or maybe some other people for some reason were laughing. I filled out the blanks and went forward to the desk. The man I had to deal with was eager to make me sign for a residence permit for one year as far as I could see. However, I felt I had to fill out the phone number and address of my guarantors. Now, obviously, this wasn't necessary, but I wanted to act correctly so I drove home to my mother's apartment to collect necessary facts linked to those guarantors of mine who also happened to be my relatives, those relatives of mine living in the USA. However, when I then later went back to the US Embassy a second time, then I didn't get any entry visa at all... if I was going on my own.

I looked at the clerk in front of me who looked back at me and asked: 'There was no problem getting a visa just two days ago. How odd! I want to talk with the US ambassador, Pontius Pilatus.'

The clerk: 'I'll tell you if you are going with some group, a research group maybe from that Monte Fresco University, a university to which you still are related, then you will be able to get any entry visa and a residence permit.' The handsome clerk now looked like a Jesus version of Richard Geere because he understood my sufferings.

I said; "I take it to your US Ambassador Pontius Pilatus to wash his hands of this dirty state of things where I can't travel freely... and will have no part of it and therefore there is a dead idea for one to try to contact your ambassador. My case is obviously an issue for the representatives of the Swedish people... they have to decide! Not Pontius Pilatus, your American ambassador here in Sweden."

Hmm, the US embassy had changed its mind in two days, I thought. From Monday to Wednesday, I thought. I clenched my fist and mumbled some hard words like: "Caramba! Rio Grande, here I come."

The clerk... was somewhat disturbed when I left. He suddenly got a long face too. Maybe... that clerk gringo realized my new solidarity with the Mexican people. Hmm, now some relatives of mine like for instance cousin Eleonor visited me... and this cousin of mine is a nurse now advised me to go to the Swedish political party and ask the people there for some assistance, etc. Yes, I had to put up with such pieces of advice from this cousin of mine named Eleonor who was a nurse and who, I was sure, was manipulated. Hmm, Eleonor had also forgotten all about a certain IB affair related to political espionage... like most Swedes or almost all Swedes... In the mid-eighties.

I also got several such pieces of advice from my other relatives, and one such other relative was an aunt of mine named Gusti... and some pieces or pieces of advice did I get, also from her... when I visited her apartment. According to this my aunt Gusti... now had relatives being related to the Swedish Employers Federation, SEF. Aunt Gusti hated that red Swedish socialist and prime minister Olof Palme and wanted to see him killed. Hmm, she had got a letter from Venezuela where her daughter stayed working for the Swedish Embassy there. Yes, this Aunt Gusti was also influenced by some people... being linked to SAF. I wrote some answers to some female contact ads, but nothing happened. Then I wrote a letter to Britain... to a penfriend club named "Global Penfriends". I had to wait two months for a list of addresses. Hmm, I chose to write and address my letters... to a woman named Brenda Foolbottle, some kind of manager at a winery and wine shop named Gallion Wine situated in or at a place called Todmorden, just outside Sheffield. Hmm, Gallion Wine... nice name. I and Brenda Foolbottle started to exchange letters, letters which often were delayed. At first, I thought that I perhaps should visit this Brenda Foolbottle, but my car didn't start. I guessed that I was the victim of some sabotage. Yes, I was obviously not allowed to leave this country Sweden, not alone. Swedish authorities wanted to be in control or could it be some other reason?

I think I had to change contact breaker points when it comes to that car of mine.. and then I got second thoughts about leaving Sweden... and one day my American cousin Folke Nyberg, arrived. Pretty soon after Folke's arrival; I and my cousin Folke were going for a car drive. We went to "The North Churchyard" where I parked my car.

Folke now began to take photos of the tombstones, etc. He seemed to like churchyards. I was watching him. I was bored. I said I felt I was buried alive face to face with Mr. Death inside a sepulchral chamber where all life-lines to the civilized society were cut off. Folke laughed when I said that. I and Folke continued to walk around taking photos of tombs and mausoleums. Folke walked around as a normal human being gladly whistling while I was coming after him staggering because I had to carry a sack named "ALL MY WORRIES MAKE ME DEPRESSED!".

While we were walking at the churchyard taking photos, I said: 'You said you came from Frankfurt. Did you happen to visit a German named Herr Beck?'

Folke just laughed. He didn't answer.

I said: 'This Herr Beck is connected to the building Research Council, BRC... just like you. You can't deny you know that manager named Ingrid Munroe, can you?'

Folke: 'Well, I have to admit that I do know Ingrid Munroe... by name. However, I won't say anything more.'

Finally, Folke's visit came to an end, but my relatives continued to drop by now and then.

Again around, for instance... my cousin Elisabeth was... after Folke's departure. Yes, my cousin Elisabeth now did visit my mother and me, at my mother's small summer cabin. We were sitting in a garden hammock, although I couldn't see much of a garden around.

Now, my cousin Elisabeth was a junior school teacher connected to the teacher's union... and now she told me just what that dubious union of school teachers wanted her to tell me. That, I was sure of... especially when Elisabeth told me to write my book in Swedish, and I should also write for small kids. Who had paid or fooled that cousin of mine to give me those pieces of bad advice, I wondered if my cousin Elisabeth also thought I should stay in my own big cabin or small house instead of being with my mother. Elisabeth obviously liked me and my manuscript to be out in the forest and when I then should have to leave all my papers of a gigantic manuscript because I had to do some shopping, etc., then my neighbor who owned a painting firm and who probably was connected to SAF being that umbrella organization regarding negotiations for different commercial corporative... then that neighbor of mine could pay my cabin or small house a visit and take a look at my manuscript. Hmm, some special pieces of bad advice from my cousin Elisabeth who were running the errands of the big and powerful ones and who also looked after her own interests being therefore not interested in my possibilities to succeed. Interesting! Besides, I didn't want to be tied up with a Swedish publisher, a Swedish publisher who might be afraid to be exposed to harassment from the Swedish authorities who in their turn were under the influence of Swedish Big Business. Yes, a Swedish publisher is afraid of being harassed by Swedish authorities, if he or should dare to publish my book, but of course, he or she could only buy a right to publish my book. Yes, and then leave it at that...

When I told my cousin, Elisabeth, that I didn't trust her or anybody else...then she recommended me a psychiatrist she knew, telling me that I did suffer from paranoia. I thought if Dr. Rinnan. No such things could ever happen in a democracy like Sweden, the best in the world, I was told. I was also told that everybody was nice and well-meaning and that the sun was shining and that we in Sweden had to trust each other and other nonsense and balderdash which my cousin Elisabeth had been informed about... by the Swedish authorities. Hmm, that pack of Swedish teachers, always running the errands of the Swedish establishment... in the early mid-eighties.

I suddenly one day heard and found a letter in this mail drop... a letter coming to my mother's apartment from this director general of the Swedish Labor Exchange, Allan Larson, telling me I could appeal against this decision of my lost wage amount & insured being rightly mine and not paid out or redeemed. Hmm, probably the calculation situation had changed for those people in power... in Sweden. We have to review the situation... they obviously now say as did once also some Literary Charles Dickensfiggis like that criminal Mr. Feign, I thought. I didn't appeal, because I knew that Swedish authorities and institutions and Swedish corporative should be trying to ensnare me.

I was now a dissenter in a criminal society with small odds to fight back. I did shiver with fear. I did also watch a demonstration against the wage taker funds and Olof Palme. There was hate in the air. Gee, there was a threat against this in Sweden not mentioned but nevertheless existing, corporative balance. Things may happen when this story continues.

Yes, my story has to go on, but let's recall what has happened so far. I was looking for solidarity, and I fixed actually two decisions which meant that some people acknowledge my weaknesses and that I was able to do some investigation. However, the decisions were regarded as an act of unfair competition... and therefore none of the two decisions were executed. Now, I experienced an arranged situation... of no work tasks, and when work tasks, then there was nothing new for me to learn. I was judged in some non-objective way, and I had to leave the university. I had no employment and recommendations, but I had something to write about in my mother's apartment. Yes, an arranged situation where I had to wait for drops of information... which made me write some more books. I think all this was criminal and criminal within the framework of some criminal experiment sanctioned by psychopaths.

Yes, I was part of an arranged situation from... or of which... it was hard to get out. Now, this arranged situation gave also fuel to a medial calumny campaign with allusions to my person... some Mr. Celebrity Concealed on Elk. Yes, there was a bounty on elks... and on me, while my social life was destroyed... and it was all very funny! Well, maybe there should be a bounty on Swedish politicos and union people and businessmen as well like for example Olof Palme and Anna Lind... Funny? Yes, some calumny campaign with allusions to me... maybe within a framework of a sick experiment... sanctions by some psychopaths... Yes, where the end results of the sick experiment could be that the test person could become some nursery object or the test person could commit suicide, or the test person could become or act as a parrot for those people in power. Hmm, why this terrible sick experiment? Well, if people like me to try take advantage of the law to hundred percent by arguing for decisions based on the Law favoring themselves and myself, then the compelling is out of joint... and then I as a troublemaker... is the man who must set it back again. However, when I shall be able to publish my writing works, then I am afraid that the Swedish publishing houses and publishing firms are also part of the centralized Swedish media apparatus and propaganda apparatus, and then I have to flee abroad in order to get published in a reasonable way. Still, the Swedes may perhaps have some first option on my book manuscripts?... Gee, criminal calumny based on some criminal cruel arranged situation being assumed to create self-censorship... and washed manuscripts... and non-existing marketing! Interesting! However, my story has to go on... since further investigations must be done.

EPILOGUE OF VOLUME III

by

Lars Warner

EPILOGUE

It was due to criminal Swedish abuse of power... that I was driven into the arms of the Americans. I then adopted quite easily the American point of view when it came to world politics. I closed my eyes when those American points of view were "just a little bit too" one-eyed or stereotyped. I decided that I should be loyal to the Americans as long as they were loyal to me... Hmm, I had a sinking feeling that some Americans didn't tell me everything... and that some Americans could use me in a scary way.

Well, and then I also had a halfway sinking feeling that Sunway Sweetiepie did know about those not-so-visible conditions which I had to face, but she didn't tell me... was this because I could be better off... or that she could be better off... or that somebody else could be better off... and was it at all someone who could be worse off?

EPILOGUE OF TOM 1

by Lars Werner

EPILOGUE I

One has to observe that Noman Skeleton (himself) voluntarily looked for help and found MAD Clinic and BAD Department and then when things didn't work out as they should Noman Skeleton played along... making observations and writing. Personal employment for Noman Skeleton at BAD Department/Monte Fresco University deliberately delayed the investigation process/employment period... Yes, and then at BAD Department and when writing Noman Skeleton has faced a lack of information and criminal demand related to sex and trafficking.

EPILOGUE II

Now, this Noman Skeleton has overheard something giving reasons to believe or he has understood that some Americans have bribed people at BAD Department... so he=Noman should be kicked out without recommendations which should give him no income and... and leave Noman to blind traveling in Europe in some maybe sexy way... if not writing, but then Noman lacks information. Hmm, at Monte Fresco University there were some indications like suggestions or extortions to fix a passport and to do some traveling to Greece/Korfu/Rhodes and such indications have it that blind sexy traveling was arranged. However, while still persisting to write Noman got waiting and waited, and finally media signals about the smuggling of weapons and smuggling of high-tech. Noman was in some informal way contracted this way... by some Americans through the Swedes after criminal negotiations. However, Noman did and obviously should still be in want of information. Hmm, a trial of what has happened and happen inside and around the BAD Department is needed to put an end to criminal calumny and slander... Hmm, American bribes with a maybe intentional sexy purpose and some maybe unintentional purpose related to crime provocation! But who can prove what in a trial?

EPILOGUE III

Well, a relief work should in theory consider my weaknesses... and one way to do it was to keep me idle and another way was to give me work tasks which they and I already know I could do. No work tests and feedback information. The result of all this was gossip and calumny, but responsible people put their heads in the "Sand" like oistrich... oistrich-people.

Well, if there is a will somewhere to avoid a problem and not solve that problem... there is a way. Hmm, solidarity is a complicated thing where many interests are involved... natural interests organized in corporative and an individual who should get help can instead be excommunicated be destroyed because of ulterior motives after criminal corporative negotiations where truth can be bent so black can become white...